# A Descriptive Guide to the English Lakes and Adjacent Mountains

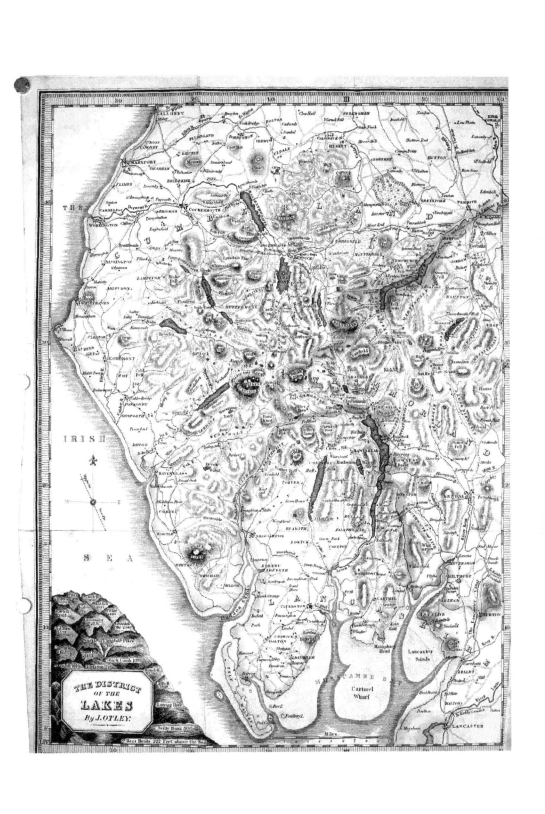

THE DISTRICT
OF THE
LAKES
By J. OTLEY.

A

# DESCRIPTIVE GUIDE

TO THE

# ENGLISH LAKES,

AND ADJACENT

# MOUNTAINS:

WITH NOTICES OF THE

Botany, Mineralogy, and Geology of the District.

## BY JONATHAN OTLEY.

SEVENTH EDITION.

TO WHICH IS ADDED,

## AN EXCURSION THROUGH LONSDALE TO THE CAVES.

KESWICK:
PUBLISHED BY THE AUTHOR;
BY SIMPKIN, MARSHALL, & CO., STATIONERS' COURT, LONDON;
AND ARTHUR FOSTER, KIRKBY LONSDALE.
1843.

# PREFACE.

GUIDES and Tours to the Lakes have been, and continue to be, offered to the Public in various forms and sizes; but chiefly devoted to a single object—the picturesque appearance of the Country—to the exclusion of other important considerations.

It is admitted, that the gratification of the eye is a leading motive with many of those who make the Tour of the Lakes; but it is not so with all. The reflecting mind will feel more satisfaction in having gained some knowledge of the structure, the natural history and productions of the region he has visited.

As a resident among the objects he attempts to describe, the Author of this Manual has possessed many opportunities of making observations, which would escape the notice of the transient visitor—the compiler from the works of others—or even of one who undertook a tour for the especial purpose of making a book.

Availing himself of these advantages, and a little experience in surveying, he constructed a Map of the District, divested of many errors which have been copied into former maps, and containing some particulars not to be found in any other. This Map, which has been re-engraved for this edition, with considerable improvements, has been accompanied with such descriptions, directions, and remarks, as were judged likely to be serviceable to the Tourist; in conducting him through the most eligible paths for viewing the varied scenery, and at the same time conveying some information on the structure and phenomena of these interesting regions.

The Lakes have been so often and so copiously dilated upon, that a concise description of them is all that has been thought necessary; but the observations upon the different Mountains are extended to some length, as they have been hitherto very inadequately and often very inaccurately described.

The Public have so far appreciated his labours as to enable him to dispose of six editions, every one of which has been carefully revised, and interspersed with additional matter, but the original design has never been departed from—to supply as much information as possible, without making the book either cumbious or expensive.

In some former editions has been introduced a series of sketches, by the Author's own unpractised hand, of the most remarkable Ranges of Mountains surrounding the different Lakes, as they appear from select stations on the roads, or places easy of access. This has been found a more intelligible mode of communicating their names than any verbal description, more easily remembered, and to obviate the necessity of many questions, often wished to be put when no one is at hand to answer. In the present edition, this department has been considerably extended, and the execution intrusted to experienced artists; and if the pains taken in collecting and arranging these materials is equalled by the reception it meets with, the Author's anticipations will be realized.

To this edition has been superadded an Excursion through the Vale of Lune, and to the Caves of the West-Riding of Yorkshire.

GOLDSMITH advised an author not to presume upon the continuance of his reputation unless he continued to be read for Ten Years.

OTLEY's GUIDE TO THE LAKES has been read for more than Twenty Years—has reached a Seventh Edition, and still continues to be read. Originally composed from personal observation, each succeeding edition has been carefully revised, interspersed with additional matter, and printed under the superintendence of the Author; who trusts that his production will not yet suffer in comparison with any rival publication.

Keswick,
  March 28th, 1845.

# CONTENTS.

# EXPLANATION OF THE MAP.

---

THE BOUNDARIES OF COUNTIES, where not formed by streams . . . } *are marked by small dots.*

TURNPIKE ROADS, . *by strong double lines.*

OTHER CARRIAGE ROADS, *by smaller double lines.*

INFERIOR CARRIAGE ROADS, *by a line on one side.*

HORSE TRACKS, OR BRIDLE ROADS, . . . } *by double lines of longish dots.*

FOOT PATHS, . . *by single lines of the same.*

NAMES OF MARKET TOWNS, *in Roman Capitals.*

PARISHES AND TOWNSHIPS, *in Italic Capitals.*

MOUNTAINS AND RIVERS, *in small Roman.*

CHURCHES AND CHAPELS, *are denoted by small crosses.*

COUNTRY INNS AND PUBLIC HOUSES, . . . } *by an open square.*

WATERFALLS, . . { *by a few strokes on each side of the stream.*

LOUGHRIGG TARN, WITH LANGDALE PIKES.

# THE LAKES.

---

THE Mountainous District in which the English Lakes are situated, extends into three Counties, Cumberland, Westmorland, and Lancashire, which form their junction at a point denoted by three shire stones, upon the mountain Wrynose, near the road side. Lancashire is separated from Cumberland by the river Duddon; from Westmorland by the stream running through Little Langdale, and by Elterwater and Windermere, until south of Storrs Hall; after which the river Winster forms the boundary till it enters the sands near Methop. Westmorland is parted from Cumberland by the mountain ridge leading over Bowfell to Dunmail Raise, and from thence over the top of Helvellyn; then by the stream of Glencoin to Ullswater, and by the river Eamont till it enters the Eden. Windermere Lake is said to belong to

Westmorland, at least its islands are claimed by
that county, although the whole of its western and
part of its eastern shores belong to Lancashire.
Coniston and Esthwaite Lakes, with Blelham and
the tarns of Coniston, are wholly in Lancashire.
Grasmere, Rydal, and Hawes Water, with several
tarns, lie in Westmorland.  The head of Ullswater
is in Westmorland, but below Glencoin it constitutes the boundary between that county and Cumberland.   Derwent, Bassenthwaite, Buttermere,
Ennerdale, and Wastwater, are in Cumberland.

Before this country became so much the resort
of strangers, the word LAKE was little known to
the native inhabitants; but to the ancient termination *mere*, WATER was usually superadded, as
Windermere Water, Grasmere Water.

## WINDERMERE

Having given its name to the adjoining parish,
it has been thought necessary, in speaking of the
lake itself, to add the word *water*, or *lake*, by way
of distinction.   It is the largest of the English
Lakes, being upwards of ten miles in length, measured upon the water; by the road on its banks,
considerably more.   Its greatest breadth is about
a mile, and depth nearly forty fathoms.

Several promontories push into the lake from
each side; and between two of these, near the

middle of its length, is a public ferry, on the road from Kendal to Hawkshead.

The numerous islands with which it is enriched, are chiefly grouped near the middle of the lake; admitting ample scope for the exercise of sailing. The principal, called Belle-Isle—in compliment to the late Mrs. Curwen, who purchased it into the family—is a beautiful plot of thirty acres, surmounted by a stately mansion, and encircled by a gravel walk of nearly two miles, which strangers, in quest of the variegated surrounding scenery, are freely permitted to perambulate. Besides this, are Crow-Holm, two Lily of the Valley-Holms, Thompson's-Holm, House-Holm, Hen-Holm, Lady-Holm, and Rough-Holm; and to the south of the Ferry, Berkshire-Island, Ling-Holm, Grass-Holm, Silver-Holm, and Blake-Holm.

Windermere is stocked with a variety of fish, of which char are the most esteemed. Char, being taken by nets in the winter months, are potted, and sent to different parts of the kingdom. The principal feeders of the lake are the Rothay, having its source in Grasmere; and the Brathay, issuing from Langdale. These two rivers unite their streams about half a mile before entering the lake; and a remarkable circumstance is, that the trout and char, both leaving the lake about the same time, to deposit their spawn, separate themselves into the two different rivers; the char making choice of the Brathay, and the trout taking to the Rothay.

This lake is situated in a country finely diversified by sloping hills, woods, and cultivated grounds, with lofty mountains in the distance. Its banks are adorned with buildings, which combine better with the scenery of this, than they would with that of the more northern lakes.

Storrs-Hall, late the mansion of Colonel Bolton, is beautifully situated upon a low promontory, and Rayrigg upon a bay of the lake. Calgarth-Park, formerly the residence of the late Bishop of Llandaff, has a lowly, and Elleray, for some time the abode of Professor Wilson, an elevated situation. The villa of Mr. Redmayne, at Brathay, and that of Mr. Brancker, at Croft-Lodge, are conspicuous objects near the head of the water.

The *Station*, belonging to Mr. Curwen, is a building erected upon a rocky eminence above the Ferry house. The path leading to it is decorated with native and exotic trees and shrubs; the upper story commands extensive views of the lake and surrounding scenery: and the windows, being partly of stained glass, give a good representation of the manner in which the landscape would be affected in different seasons. The view towards the north has every essential for a beautiful landscape: a bold foreground, a fine sheet of water, graced with islands, the large one, belonging to Mr. Curwen, with its dome-topped building, being a principal feature; the village of Bowness, the mansions placed at various points, the rich woods, and distant mountains, all contribute to enrich the

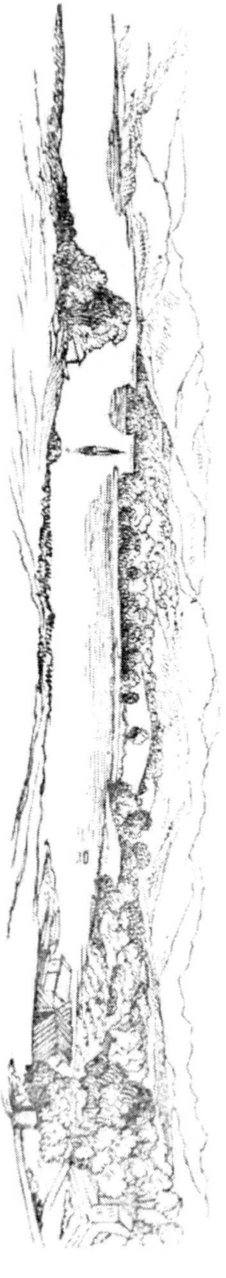

WINDERMERE:— *Looking towards the North-East.*

FROM BOWNESS.

...High Raise

...Ullskarth, Wythburn Head

...Stile

...Loughrigg Fell (line 2)
...[Raise Gap]

...Gilbert Scar (line 2)

...Nab Scar

...Great Rigg

...Fairfield

...[Rydal Park]

...Wansfell Pike

...Red Screes, near Kirkstone

...Woundale Head

Troutbeck Hundreds (1.2)

...Cawdale Moor

...Threshthwaite Mouth

...High Street

...Froswick

...Ill Bell

...Yoak
...Applethwaite Fell

scene. The southern half of the lake is narrower; but its shores are beautifully broken and wooded.

Some would like to commence their survey of Windermere at Newby Bridge, and observe the scenery unfolding itself as they advance. Others will be more gratified by the prospect bursting upon them at once, in full expansion, as it does from the elevated ground, on either of the roads leading from Kendal towards Bowness or Ambleside. All the way, from two miles south of Bowness, to the head of the lake, the views are excellent; and every rising ground affords something new in the combination. Rayrigg-Bank has the most complete view of the whole lake, from north to south; but a station about a mile from Low Wood Inn, on the highest part of the road towards Troutbeck, being more elevated, gives the most distinct view of all the islands, and the spaces between them. About Troutbeck Bridge, the range of mountains, extending from Coniston Old Man to Langdale Pikes, appears to great advantage: the Pikes, on Scawfell, (the highest land in England,) being seen on the left of Bowfell; and, between it and Langdale Pikes, stand Great End and Gable, as if guarding the pass at Sty-Head. From some parts of the lake the summit of Helvellyn can just be seen, beyond the fells of Grasmere and Rydal. It may also be seen from the top of Brantfell, and from a rocky knoll lower down; and a peep at Skiddaw is obtained at the junction of the Cartmel and Milnthorpe roads, a mile and a half south of Bowness.

A walk, or a ride, along the sequestered road from the Ferry towards Ambleside, will be found agreeable to the contemplative mind; and during a voyage on the northern part of the lake—without which no tour can be called complete—a variety of both near and distant scenes are presented to the view in delightful succession: the different vallies being opened out to the eye of the spectator in a manner unequalled from any station. As the boat proceeds from the landing place at Low Wood, a person, previously acquainted with the distant mountains, will feel a pleasure in observing how the highest Pike on Scawfell seems to march forth from behind Bowfell, and the Gable from behind Langdale Pikes.

Bowness is an irregularly built but very neat village, on the banks of the lake; it has two splendid inns, and one of a secondary description; and there are several genteel residences in the neighbourhood. Low Wood Inn stands sweetly at the edge of the water; and Ambleside is at a convenient distance for making excursions, either upon the lake, or to the adjacent vallies and mountains.

At Newby Bridge, on the foot of the lake, is an inn, where boats and post-horses may be had; another at the Ferry, on the Lancashire side; and the inns at Bowness, Low Wood, and Ambleside are spacious, and furnished with every requisite accommodation.

WINDERMERE:—*Looking towards the West.*

FROM THE ROAD BETWEEN TROUTBECK BRIDGE AND BOWNESS.

...Old Man—Coniston Fell

...The Carrs

...Wetherlam

...[Wrynose Gap]

...Pike of Bliscow (line 2)
...Crinkle Crags

...Scawfell Pike

...Bowfell

...Great End
...Lingmoor (line 2)
...Hindside
...Great Gable
...Pike of Stickle

...Harrison Stickle

...Paveyark

...High Raise

...Silverhow (line 2)

...Hammerscar (line 2)

## ESTHWAITE WATER

Is a small placid lake, nearly two miles in length, and distinguished by a fine swelling peninsula, which reaches far into the water from the western side. It is situated near the ancient little town of Hawkshead, in a beautiful open valley, which is crowned with gentle eminences, and decorated with an agreeable composition of houses, fields, and trees.

On a pond called Priest Pot, near the head of this lake, there is a Floating Island, 24 yards in length, and 5 or 6 in breadth, supporting several alder and willow trees of considerable size. Differing from the one in Derwent lake, which rises occasionally from the bottom, this remains always upon the surface, generally resting against the shore; but, when the water is high, it is sometimes moved from side to side by a change of wind; and, by such means, has undoubtedly been torn from the bank at some remote period.

A gentleman, trolling in Esthwaite Water, seven days in May last, caught the unprecedented number of 130 pike, averaging in weight about 2lbs.

## GRASMERE LAKE

Is not large, but well formed; and placed near the confines of a cultivated valley, which, with the parish, takes the name of Grasmere. The island, containing about four acres of verdant pasture, forms a striking contrast to the massively wooded islands on some of the neighbouring lakes. It rises boldly from the water, in a fine swelling form;

and its smooth green surface, when spotted with
cattle grazing, has a beautiful appearance.   Most
of the lakes, in order to be seen to advantage,
require the progress to be made from the foot
towards the head of the lake; but Grasmere, being
completely encircled by mountains, is an exception
to the general rule.   The view from Dunmail
Raise was much admired by Mr. Gray; others
have spoken highly of that from Townend; and
Mr. West chose his station on Dearbought hill,
at the head of Red Bank, on the opposite side.
In short, from whatever point the approach to
Grasmere is made, the prospect is always pleasing.

There are two good houses for the accommodation of travellers: the Red Lion, supplying post
horses and jaunting cars, is near the Church; and
the Swan on the turnpike road.

## RYDAL WATER

Is of smaller dimensions, and formed in a more
contracted part of the valley; it receives the river
flowing from Grasmere lake after a course of about
half-a-mile.   It is ornamented by two picturesque
islands, on one of which the herons build their
nests in the trees; and it is bordered by meadows
and woody grounds, surmounted on one side by
the precipitous rocks of Nab Scar, and on the
other by the steeps of Loughrigg Fell.

The fish in Grasmere and Rydal Waters are
pike, perch, (provincially called bass,) and eels,
with a few trout.

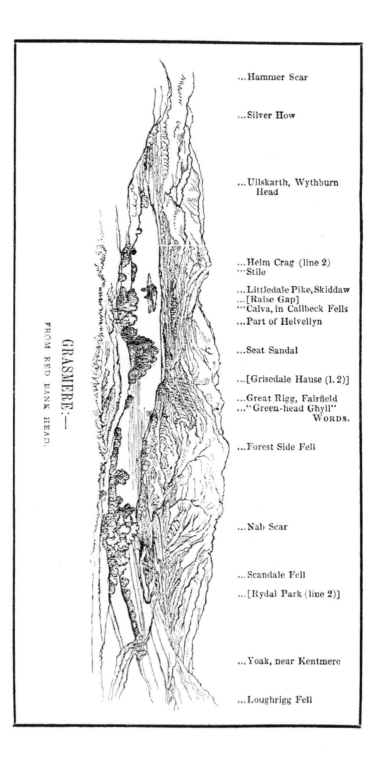

GRASMERE:—

FROM RED BANK HEAD.

...Hammer Scar

...Silver How

...Ullskarth, Wythburn Head

...Helm Crag (line 2)
···Stile
...Littledale Pike, Skiddaw
...[Raise Gap]
···Calva, in Callbeck Fells
...Part of Helvellyn

...Seat Sandal

...[Grisedale Hause (1. 2)]

...Great Rigg, Fairfield
..."Green-head Ghyll"
                    WORDS.

...Forest Side Fell

...Nab Scar

...Scandale Fell

...[Rydal Park (line 2)]

...Yoak, near Kentmere

...Loughrigg Fell

# THIRLMERE

—Commonly called LEATHES' WATER, from the family to whose estate it belongs, and sometimes WYTHBURN WATER, from the valley in which it is partly situated—lies at the foot of the "mighty Helvellyn;" upon the highest level of any of the lakes, being nearly 500 feet above the sea; it is upwards of two miles and a-half in length, and intersected by several rocky promontories; it is divided into an upper and lower lake, between which a picturesque wooden bridge leads to Armboth House. The depth of this lake, which has been reported to be very great, has not been found to exceed eighteen fathoms. A wooded island, of half an acre, lies near the shore, on the lower or northern part of the lake; and the surface of the water being of late somewhat lowered by opening its outlet, a small rock in the upper part has become more conspicuous.

Travellers are commonly satisfied with a sight of this lake from the road; but those who have leisure may obtain better views of the lower and finer part of the lake, from different stations in the grounds near Dalehead House; and the upper part of the lake, with its mountains, is best seen by those who turn off near the fourth mile stone, and travel the western side of the water. But the most perfect view of the whole lake is from a rocky eminence at a little distance from its northern end.

## CONISTON WATER,

Called in some old books THURSTON WATER, is a lake of considerable magnitude, being six miles in length; but wanting in that agreeable flexure of shores so conducive to the beauty of a lake. Near its foot, however, are some finely wooded, rocky promontories; which, from certain points, add greatly to the prospect. It has two small islands, but they are placed too near the shore to contribute much to its importance.

As the principal mountains lie on the western side and at its head, the best views are in consequence obtained in a progress from its foot, on the eastern side, or from a boat on its surface; but those who have leisure may be gratified by the variety afforded in an excursion quite round the lake.

Its greatest depth is twenty-seven fathoms. It is well supplied with trout and char; the latter are said to be better here than in any other lake; they are taken by nets in winter, and it was formerly supposed they could not be tempted by any kind of bait; however, they are sometimes taken by angling, with a hook baited in a peculiar manner with a minnow.

The inn, at Waterhead, is pleasantly situated on the margin of the lake, and furnishes parties with pleasure boats, a chaise, and pair of post horses.

Waterhead House, the property and occasional residence of James Marshall, Esq., stands delightfully on a rising ground a short distance from the inn.

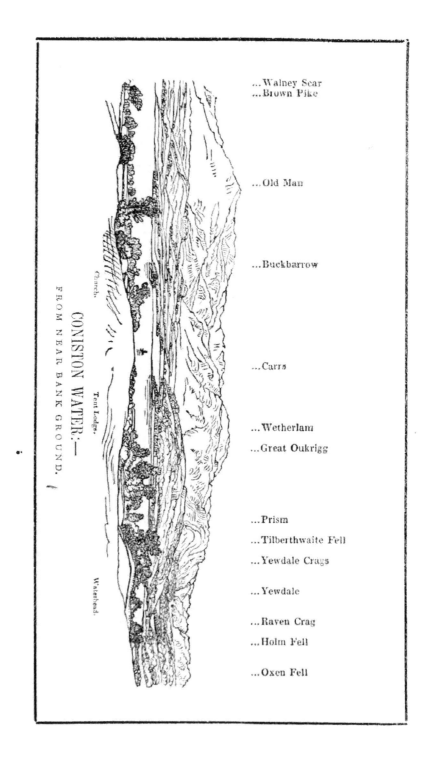

CONISTON WATER:—
FROM NEAR BANK GROUND.

Church.

Tent Lodge.

Waterhead.

...Walney Scar
...Brown Pike

...Old Man

...Buckbarrow

...Carrs

...Wetherlam

...Great Oukrigg

...Prism

...Tilberthwaite Fell

...Yewdale Crags

...Yewdale

...Raven Crag

...Holm Fell

...Oxen Fell

## DERWENT LAKE,

Near Keswick, is of the most agreeable proportions. In breadth, it exceeds any of the neighbouring lakes, being nearly a mile and a half; although its whole length is little more than three miles. Lakes of greater length generally extend too far from that mountain scenery, which is so conducive to their importance; but Derwent lake appears wholly surrounded; and visitors are at a loss which to admire most, the broken rocky mountains of Borrowdale on the one hand, or the smooth flowing lines of Newlands on the other; while the majestic Skiddaw closes up the view to the north.

The islands are of a more proportionate size, and disposed at better distances, than those in any of the neighbouring lakes. The largest, called Lord's Isle, contains about six acres and a half, and is covered with stately trees, forming a fine rookery. It is situated near the shore, on which account, probably, it was selected for the residence of the family of Derwentwater; but the house has long been in ruins, and nothing now remains but the foundation. This, and the smaller island called Rampsholm, form part of the late Earl of Derwentwater's sequestrated estate, which was purchased from Greenwich Hospital, in 1832, by the late John Marshall, jun., Esq., of Leeds.

The Vicar's Isle, the residence of James Henry, Esq., contains about six acres, beautifully laid out in pleasure grounds, interspersed with a variety of

trees, and crowned with a house in the centre.
For some years it was called Pocklington's Island,
while it belonged to a gentleman of that name;
and is now, by way of pre-eminence, styled Derwent Isle.

One, nearer the middle of the lake, is called St.
Herbert's Isle, from being the residence of that
holy man, who, according to the Venerable Bede,
was contemporary with St. Cuthbert, and died
about A.D. 687.   It appears that several centuries
afterwards, the anniversary of his death was, by
the Bishop of the diocese, enjoined to be celebrated
upon this spot in religious offices.   Some remains
of what is said to have been his cell are still to be
seen among the trees with which the island is
covered.   About 1798, a small grotto or fishing
cot was built by the late Sir Wilfred Lawson, of
Brayton House, to whose successor the island now
belongs.

There are other small islets; as Otter Isle,
situated in a bay near the head of the lake, the
views from which have been much admired; a
piece of rock called Tripetholm, and two others
known by the name of Lingholms.

Besides these permanent islands, an occasional
one is sometimes observed, called the Floating
Island: being a piece of earth, which, at uncertain
intervals of time, rises from the bottom to the surface of the lake; but still adhering by its sides to
the adjacent earth, is never removed from its
place.   Within the last thirty-five years, it has

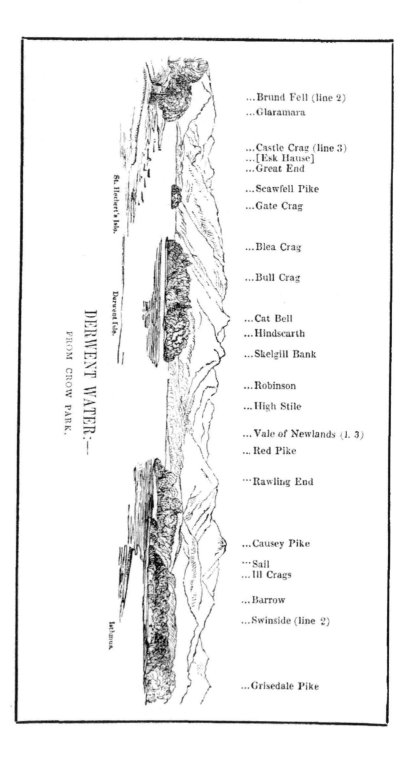

DERWENT WATER:—

FROM CROW PARK.

St. Herbert's Isle.

Derwent Isle.

Isthmus.

...Brund Fell (line 2)

...Glaramara

...Castle Crag (line 3)
...[Esk Hause]
...Great End

...Scawfell Pike

...Gate Crag

...Blea Crag

...Bull Crag

...Cat Bell

...Hindscarth

...Skelgill Bank

...Robinson

...High Stile

...Vale of Newlands (l. 3)

...Red Pike

...Rawling End

...Causey Pike

...Sail

...Ill Crags

...Barrow

...Swinside (line 2)

...Grisedale Pike

emerged twelve times; remaining upon the surface for longer or shorter periods. In a succeeding part of this work the discussion of this subject will be resumed at greater length.

The lands bordering the lake belong principally to three wealthy proprietors. The heirs of the late Mr. Marshall hold the Derwentwater estate on the east; Major-General Sir John Woodford, the late Lord William Gordon's estate on the west; and Mr. Standish, late Stephenson, chiefly the south. Mr. Pocklington's estate at Barrow also adjoins the lake, and his house boldly overlooks it. The neat cottage of Sir John Woodford is secreted by lofty woods, on the edge of a placid bay, on the western side of the lake.

Derwent Lake lies 228 feet above the level of the sea; its depth does not in any part exceed fourteen fathoms: a great portion of it scarcely one fourth of that measure. It is supplied chiefly from Borrowdale, and forms a reservoir for the water, which, in heavy rains, pours down the steep mountains on every side; by which means its surface is often raised six or seven feet; and, in an extraordinary case, has been known to rise a perpendicular height of eight feet, above its lowest water mark. At such times the meadows are overflowed, all the way between this lake and Bassenthwaite. Its surface being large in proportion to its depth, causes it to be sooner cooled down to the freezing point; and it frequently affords a fine field for the skaiter. In January, 1814, the ice attained the thickness of ten inches; and once or twice since that time it has nearly reached the same dimensions.

The fishery and right of navigation on the east side belongs to the Derwentwater estate; on the west, to the Earl of Egremont; and on the south, to the freeholders of Borrowdale. The fish are trout, pike, perch, and eels. The trout, which are very good, are taken by angling, in the months of April and May; the pike and perch, during the whole summer.

It would be superfluous to enter into a description or enumeration of the different views on this lake: many attempts have been made to describe them—but they must be seen to be duly appreciated.

Parties navigating the lake may be landed to view the cascades at Barrow and Lowdore: at the latter place is a public-house, where a cannon is kept for the echo, which on a favourable opportunity is very fine; the sound being reverberated from the rocks encompassing the valley, at intervals proportioned to their respective distances.

To such as have not another opportunity of viewing the scenery of Borrowdale, it may be recommended to leave the boat at Lowdore, and to walk forward to Bowder Stone, a distance of two miles; where is a good prospect of the upper part of Borrowdale, with Castle Crag on the right, Eagle Crag on the left, and Great End Crag in the distance. The village of Rosthwaite, sheltered by rising hills and stately trees, on the verge of green meadows, filling up the middle space.

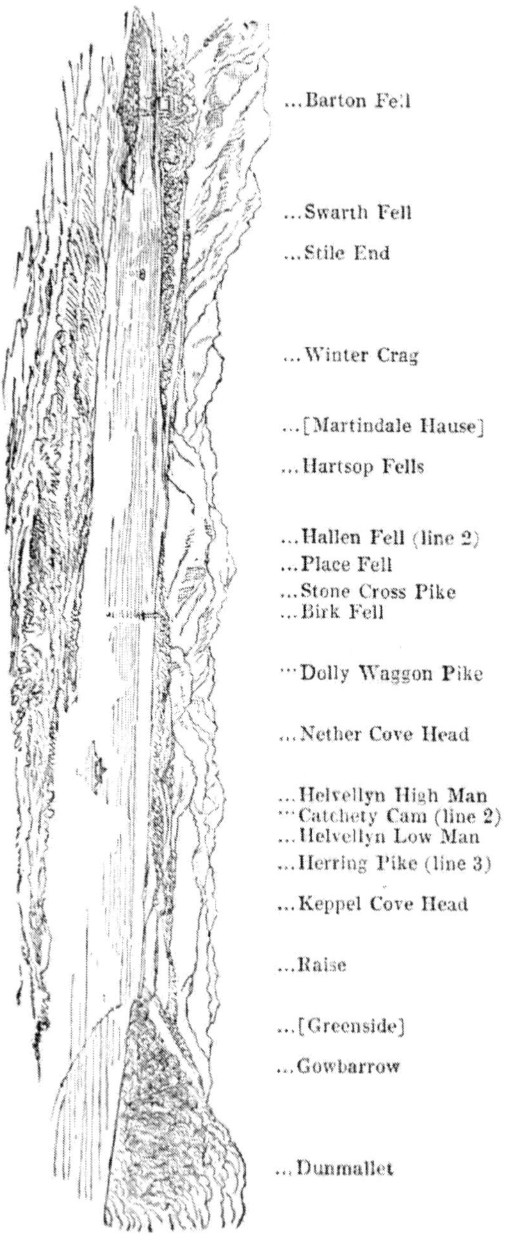

ULLSWATER:—

FROM POOLEY BRIDGE.

...Barton Fell

...Swarth Fell

...Stile End

...Winter Crag

...[Martindale Hause]

...Hartsop Fells

...Hallen Fell (line 2)
...Place Fell
...Stone Cross Pike
...Birk Fell

...Dolly Waggon Pike

...Nether Cove Head

...Helvellyn High Man
...Catchety Cam (line 2)
...Helvellyn Low Man
...Herring Pike (line 3)

...Keppel Cove Head

...Raise

...[Greenside]

...Gowbarrow

...Dunmallet

## ULLSWATER

Ranks second in point of size, being nine miles long, but rather wanting in breadth: yet, on account of its winding form, the disproportion is not so much observed. It has the greatest average depth of any of the lakes, being in many places from 20 to 35 fathoms. The country about its foot is rather tame; but its head is situated among some of the most majestic mountains, which are intersected by several glens or small vallies; and their sides embellished with a variety of native wood and rock scenery.

Three rocky islets ornament the upper reach of the lake; they are called Cherry-Holm, Wall-Holm, and House-Holm; the last of which is a fine station for viewing the surrounding country.

This lake abounds with trout, which are sometimes caught of very large size: char are likewise found, but not of the best quality. Large shoals of a peculiar kind of fish are met with, called here the skelly; and great quantities of eels are taken in the river Eamont, below Pooley Bridge, as they migrate from the lake in autumn. The foot of the lake seems to be embanked by a conglomerated mass of pebbles; the same composition forms the finely wooded hill called Dunmallet, which stands like a centinel to guard the pass. The "mighty Helvellyn," flanked right and left by subordinate mountains, is seen in the most favourable point of view from Pooley Bridge.

The borders of the lake are ornamented with several handsome villas. Ewesmere hill commands delightful prospects up the lake; Colonel Salmond's beautiful residence at Waterfoot, retires from the view; on the borders of the lake are those of Rampsbeck Beau-Thorn, Lemon-House, and Old-Church; at a little distance Watermillock; and at Hallsteads, on a fine promontory with undulating grounds, John Marshall, Esq., has an elegant house. Lyulph's Tower is a hunting box, built by the late Duke of Norfolk in his deer park; and Airey Force may be seen by application to the keeper who resides here. Glencoin is a farm placed in a sweet recess, where a brook divides the counties of Cumberland and Westmorland. At the foot of Glenridding, the Rev. H. Askew has a tasteful cottage; and towards the foot of Grisedale, the seat of W. Marshall, Esq., stands upon the site of the ancient Patterdale Hall.

The only carriage road lies on the north-west side of the water, sometimes on a level with its surface, and commanding an unobstructed view; at other times deeply shaded in ancient woods, permitting only occasional glimpses of the lake; but on the opposite side the pedestrian will be well repaid for a ramble along Placefell and Birkfell. From the slate quarry there is a grand view of the mountains, just including the highest point of Helvellyn; and from many parts of the path, and above it, the views are truly picturesque and beautiful.

If the tourist aspires to more extensive pros-

THE MOUNTAINS OF PATTERDALE:—

FROM THE SLATE QUARRY ON PLACE FELL.

The Inn.

Patterdale Hall.

...Place Fell

...Cawdale Moor
...Hartsop Dod

...[Kirkstone Pass]
...Red Screes

...[Deepdale Park]

...Blease

...Birks

...Dolly Waggon Pike

...[Grisedale]

...Eagle Crag

...Bleaberry Crag
...Helvellyn Pile

...Hall Bank (line 2)

...[Raise]

...[Glenridding]

...Greenside

...Herring Pike

...Glenridding Dod (l. 2)

spects, they may be attained by climbing the mountain to a certain height; where the lower extremity of the lake may be seen over the beautiful grounds of Hallsteads.

This lake, like others, is most advantageously seen by commencing at its foot; so that, whether by the road, or in a boat, the grandeur of the scenery is continually increasing as the traveller approaches the mountains; but the views from the lake are more open, and the water itself appears more spacious, from the boat on its surface, than from any elevation above it.

There is a comfortable inn at Pooley Bridge, on the foot of the lake; and another at Patterdale, a little distance from its head. They both furnish boats upon the lake: and the long wanted medium of land conveyance is now supplied, by horses and post chaise being furnished both at Pooley Bridge and Patterdale.

## BROTHERS WATER,

—So called from the circumstance of two brothers having been drowned together, by the breaking of the ice—is a small lake, situate in that part of Patterdale called Hartshop, on the road leading to and from Ambleside. In the latter direction, descending from the steeps of Kirkstone, its first appearance is always greeted with pleasure by the tourist in search of the picturesque; who considers it the commencement of a new series of beauties.

c 2

# HAWES WATER

Is nearly three miles in length, and half a mile in breadth; it is almost divided into two parts by the projection of a plot of cultivated land from the N. W. side. Its head is encompassed by lofty mountains, but they exhibit less variety of outline than those of Derwent and Ullswater. Its eastern side is bounded by Naddle Forest, the lower part completely wooded, and surmounted by the lofty Wallow Crag; beyond which the hill side is scattered with aged thorns. The western side has more cultivation, and a few farm houses sheltered by trees. The houses, with the exception of Mr. Boustead's, at Measand-beck, and Mr. Holmes', at Chapel hill, are mostly walled without mortar; and the deciduous trees associate well with the rest of the scenery. Opposite the head of the lake, Castle Crag is a prominent feature in the landscape.

This lake is well stocked with fish of various kinds; but they are chiefly preserved for the table of Lowther Castle.

Lying beyond the usual circuit of the lakes, and at a distance from the great roads and places of entertainment, Hawes Water is often omitted. But tourists, who can contrive to visit it without hurry or fatigue, will find it a sweet retired spot.

There is a public house at Mardale Green, about a mile above the head of the lake; and a spacious inn, with one of smaller dimensions, at Bampton Grange, a distance of two miles from its foot.

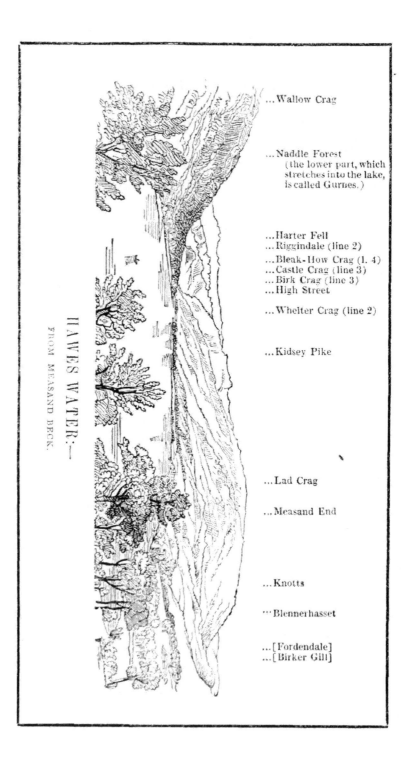

HAWES WATER:—

FROM MEASAND BECK.

...Wallow Crag

...Naddle Forest
(the lower part, which
stretches into the lake,
is called Gurnes.)

...Harter Fell
...Riggindale (line 2)
...Bleak-How Crag (l. 4)
...Castle Crag (line 3)
...Birk Crag (line 3)
...High Street

...Whelter Crag (line 2)

...Kidsey Pike

...Lad Crag

...Measand End

...Knotts

...Blennerhasset

...[Fordendale]
...[Birker Gill]

## BASSENTHWAITE LAKE

Is of somewhat greater length than Derwent, but of less breadth, and without islands. Being further from the mountains, it is not viewed with the same interest as some other lakes. Its western side is rather too uniformly wooded, the eastern has a greater breadth of cultivation, on which side are some fine bays and promontories; but here the road recedes too far from the lake to exhibit it to advantage. However, tourists who have leisure for a ride or a drive of eighteen miles, round this lake, may obtain some pleasing views; especially from the foot of the lake, and from some points of Wythop woods. This lake is of less depth than Derwent. Pike and perch are the principal fish: salmon pass through it, to deposit their spawn in the rivers Derwent and Greta, but are seldom met-with in the lake.

## BUTTERMERE LAKE,

Situate in the valley of that name, is nearly encompassed by superb rocky mountains. It is about a mile and a quarter in length, scarcely half a mile in breadth, and fifteen fathoms deep.

Tourists visiting Buttermere, by way of Borrowdale, pass along the side of this lake; those who travel in carriages generally content themselves with the view of it from a hill near the village.

# CRUMMOCK LAKE

Is nearly three miles in length, three quarters of
a mile in breadth, and twenty-two fathoms deep.
It is situated between the two lofty and precipitous mountains of Grasmoor, on the eastern,
and Melbreak, on the western side; and, in combination with the more distant hills, it makes a
beautiful picture. The best general views of the
lake are from the rocky point on the eastern side,
called the Hause; and from the road between Scale
Hill and Lowes Water: and the views of the mountains, from the bosom of the lake, are excellent.
On one side stands Grasmoor, with its lofty precipitous front; on the other, Melbreak rises ab-
ruptly from the water's edge; Whiteless Pike,
Robinson, Rannerdale Knot, Fleetworth Pike,
Honister Crag, Red Pike, High Stile, and the
Haystacks, surmounted by Great Gable, all contribute to the magnificence of the scene.

The distance between Crummock and Buttermere
Lakes is short of a mile, of excellent arable land.

Both these lakes are well stocked with trout and
char, the latter of which are smaller in size, but
perhaps not inferior in quality, to those of Windermere or Coniston. There is a comfortable inn
at Buttermere, between the two lakes, and another
at Scale Hill, on the foot of Crummock; at one of
which places a boat is usually taken, as well for a
survey of the scenery, as being the most convenient way of seeing the noted waterfall of Scale
Force, on the opposite side of the lake.

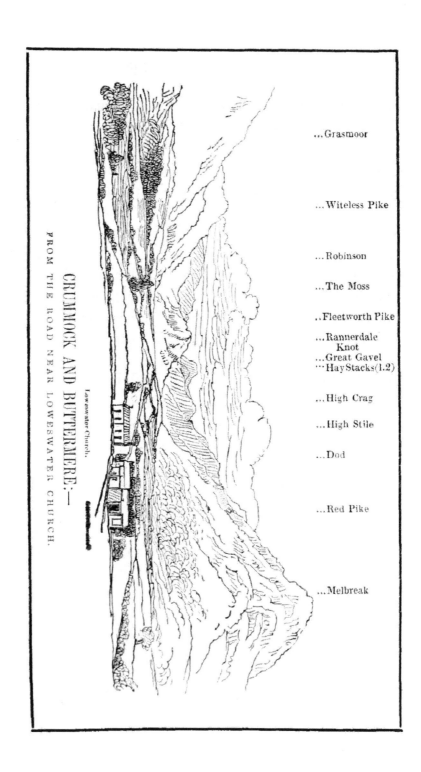

CRUMMOCK AND BUTTERMERE;—

FROM THE ROAD NEAR LOWESWATER CHURCH.

Loweswater Church.

...Grasmoor

...Witeless Pike

...Robinson

...The Moss

..Fleetworth Pike

...Rannerdale Knot
...Great Gavel
...HayStacks(1.2)

...High Crag

...High Stile

...Dod

...Red Pike

...Melbreak

## LOWES WATER,

A small lake of about a mile in length, has given name to the parochial chapelry in which it is situated. Shaping its course towards Crummock, its direction is contrary to that of the neighbouring lakes, from which it differs also, in another point: they generally exhibit the most interesting mountain scenery in looking towards the head of the lake; this, on the contrary, is more tame towards its head, while at its foot the mountains appear of bolder forms. It is not the difference between one sheet of water and another, but the endless variety of scenery with which they are associated, that gives to every lake its peculiar character. Lowes Water, viewed from the end of Melbreak, exhibits a sweet rural landscape, the cultivated slopes being ornamented with neat farm-houses and trees: but, taking the view in an opposite direction, the lake makes a middle distance to a combination of mountains scarcely to be equalled.

Parties who visit Lowes Water from Scale Hill, generally content themselves with a view from the place of its first presentation; but those who approach it from the west, have the advantage of beholding it in connection with a most magnificent assemblage of mountains. On the left, Grasmoor, Whiteless Pike, Robinson, and Rannerdale Knot; on the right, Burnbank and Carling Knot; in front, Melbreak rises in an aspiring cone, flanked by High Stile and Red Pike on one hand, and the perpendicular-fronted Honister Crag on the other.

## ENNERDALE LAKE

Is about two miles and a half in length, and three quarters of a mile in breadth. It is more difficult to obtain a good sight of this than of any other lake. The best general view may be had near How Hall; but as the principal mountain scenery, with part of the lake, is seen to advantage from the road by which tourists generally pass from Wast Water to Lowes Water and Buttermere, few like to extend their journey two or three miles for any improvement to be made in the prospect. Pedestrians, anxious to explore the inmost recesses of the mountains, may follow the lake to its head, and after passing the sequestered farm of Gillerthwaite, continue their route four or five miles along the narrow dale, by the transparent stream of the Lisa, which is fed by the crystal springs issuing from the side of the mountain; and either turn to the left, by the pass called Scarf Gap, to Buttermere; or to the right, over the Black Sail, to Wasdale Head. This way a horse might be taken, but it would be found more troublesome than useful.

This lake is well stocked with trout: here is also an inferior kind of char, which enter the river in autumn to deposit their spawn; contrary to the habits of those in the lakes of Buttermere and Crummock.

There are two small public-houses at Ennerdale Bridge; but not calculated to afford much accommodation to travellers.

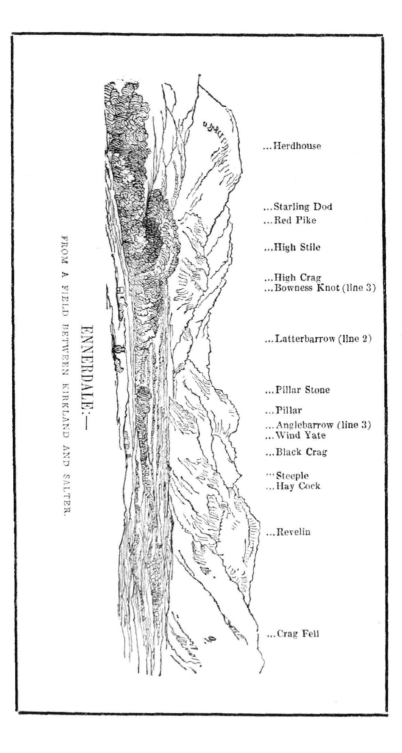

ENNERDALE:—

FROM A FIELD BETWEEN KIRKLAND AND SALTER.

...Herdhouse

...Starling Dod
...Red Pike

...High Stile

...High Crag
...Bowness Knot (line 3)

...Latterbarrow (line 2)

...Pillar Stone

...Pillar

...Anglebarrow (line 3)
...Wind Yate

...Black Crag

...Steeple
...Hay Cock

...Revelin

...Crag Fell

r

## WAST WATER

Is a lake full three miles in length, and more than half a mile in breadth. It has been recently sounded to the depth of 45 fathoms; but we have been told of a particular spot, where a line of double the length did not reach the bottom: which must at any rate be several fathoms below the level of the sea. It is probably owing to its great depth, in proportion to the extent of surface, that it has never been known to freeze; the duration of winter not being sufficient to cool the whole mass of water to that temperature which permits ice to be formed upon its surface.

The fish of Wast Water are chiefly trout, with which it is well stored: it also contains a few char. Boats are kept by neighbouring gentlemen for the diversion of angling; and the appearance of the Screes from the lake is magnificent. At Nether Wasdale, about a mile and a half from the foot of the lake, there are two public houses where travellers may have refreshment for themselves and horses: there is no other between this and Rosthwaite in Borrowdale, a distance of fourteen miles, one third of which is very difficult mountain road.

Wasdale Head consists of about half a dozen dwellings sheltered by trees, and a small Chapel, in the midst of an area of arable land, encircled by the loftiest mountains. A public house here is much wanted; the kind hospitality of the inhabi-

tants being not unfrequently drawn upon by strangers; but it is expected that a license to entertain
travellers will shortly be obtained by one of the
householders.    Bowderdale has a single farm-
house, in a lateral valley opening near the middle of the lake.    At Crook Head, near the foot
of the lake, Stansfield Rawson, Esq., of Halifax,
has a neat Gothic summer residence, called Wasdale Hall.

The mountains environing Wast Water are lofty
and majestic.   A shivery mountain side, called the
Screes, bounds the lake on the south-east, extending quite into the water; so that it cannot be
passed on that side, even by a pedestrian, without
considerable difficulty, and some danger.    From
some points of view, Yewbarrow forms a fine
apex, while Kirkfell retires behind it; at the head
of the dale the pyramidical Gable appears conspicuous; Lingmell comes boldly forward on the
right, over which Scawfell and the Pikes reign
pre-eminent; the Hay Cock may be seen through
the lateral vale of Bowderdale, and the Pillar crowns
the head of the branch called Mosedale: Middle-
fell, running along the margin of the lake on the
spectator's side, and the Screes on the opposite,
complete the panorama.   In short, Wast Water
affords many peculiarities well worth visiting once,
but scarcely sufficient to yield that increased degree of pleasure in a second and third inspection,
which would be experienced on Derwent, Ullswater, or Windermere.

MOUNTAINS OF WAST WATER:—

AS SEEN FROM NETHER WASDALE.

...Buckbarrow Pike

...Middlefell

...Yewbarrow

···Great Gable

...Sty Head Pass

...Lingmell

···Great-end Crag

...Scawfell Pike

...Scawfell

THE SCREES.

## THE TARNS.

THERE are numerous other receptacles of still water, which, being too small to merit the appellation of lakes, are called TARNS. When placed in a principal valley, (which however is not often the case,) they contribute little to its importance; and being in such situations often environed with swampy ground, seem to represent the feeble remains of a once more considerable lake. But in a circular recess on the side of a vale, or on a mountain, as they are generally placed, their margins being well defined, they become more interesting. Reposing frequently at the foot of lofty precipices, and sometimes appearing as if embanked by a collection of materials excavated from the basin which they occupy, they afford ample room for conjecture as to the mode of their formation. Being sheltered from the winds, their surface often exhibits the finest reflections of the rocks and surrounding scenery, highly pleasing to the eye of such as view them with regard to the picturesque; but it is more agreeable to the wishes of the angler, to see their surface ruffled by the breeze.

*Tarns in the tributary streams of Windermere.*

Elterwater is one of the largest of the Tarns; and having given its name to a small hamlet in Langdale, it became necessary, in speaking of the water itself, to add the word tarn by way of distinction. It is nearly a mile in length, and divided into three parts. By the sudden influx of water from the two Langdales, the low meadows on its margin are frequently overflowed, and rendered wet and swampy. To obviate this, great pains have lately been taken in opening its outlet; by which means the dimensions of the water have been greatly contracted; and the fishery of trout has been nearly annihilated by the introduction of that voracious fish, the pike.——Loughrigg Tarn is a circular piece of water of about twenty acres, environed by green meadows, intermixed with rocky woods and cultivated grounds. Its glassy surface displays beautiful reflections of the farm-houses, fields, and trees, surmounted by rocky steeps; and when taken in combination with Langdale Pikes in the distance, it makes an excellent picture.——Little Langdale Tarn, in the valley of that name, is one whose consequence is lessened by the swampiness of its shores.——Blea Tarn, lying on the high ground between the two vales of Great and Little Langdale, has a small sequestered farm adjoining, which is called by its name. A view of this piece of water is enriched by the superb appearance of Langdale Pikes.—— Stickle Tarn, at the foot of Pavey-ark, a huge rock in connection with Langdale Pikes, is famous for the quality of its trout. Its dimensions have been greatly enlarged by its adaption as a reservoir for the gunpowder mills at Elterwater. The stream falling into Langdale, at Millbeck, in a foaming cataract, may be seen at a distance.——Codale Tarn is a small piece of water, containing a few trout, perch, and eels. It sends a small stream down a rocky channel into Easdale Tarn, which is one of the largest mountain tarns, seated in the western branch of Grasmere vale, among rocky precipices, of which Blakerigg, or Blea Crag, is the principal. Its stream is, from its frothy whiteness, called Sourmilk Gill, and, when well supplied with water, is a striking object from the road.

### Tarns in the environs of Ullswater.

Ayes Water is of more extended dimensions than most of those called tarns; and is much frequented by anglers. The stream from it passes Low Hartshop, joining that from Brothers Water near the foot of the latter.——Angle Tarn, lying north of the last, upon the mountain separating Patterdale from Martindale, is one of the smaller class; but of a curious shape, having two rocky islets, and a small broken peninsula. Its stream, in a quick descent, reaches the vale about half a mile further down.—— Grisedale Tarn, one of the larger class, lies in the junction of the three mountains, Helvellyn, Seatsandal,* and Fairfield. The

* The rain water falling upon Seatsandal, runs into Windermere, Ullswater, and Derwent, entering the sea by the river Leven into Morecambe Bay; by the Eden into the Solway Frith; and by the Derwent into the Irish Sea.

road over the Hause, from Grasmere to Patterdale, passing the tarn, is accompanied by its stream down the vale of Grisedale, which unites with the parent valley near the Church.——Red Tarn, also of considerable extent, containing upwards of twenty acres, is upon the highest level of any of the mountain tarns; being upwards of two thousand three hundred feet above the level of the sea, and about seven hundred feet below the summit of Helvellyn; from whence into it you might almost cast a stone.——Keppel Cove Tarn is posited in a singular manner, not in the bottom of the glen, but in a kind of recess formed on one side; it is separated from Red Tarn by a narrow mountain ridge called Swirrel Edge, which branches off from Helvellyn and is terminated by a peak called Catsty Cam, modernized into Catchedecam; below which the two streams unite to form the brook of Glenridding. All these tarns afford good diversion for the angler: Keppel Cove produces a bright, well shapen trout; those of Angle Tarn are by some considered of superior flavour; but when quantity as well as quality is taken into account, Ayes Water may perhaps be allowed the pre-eminence.

### Tarns connected with Hawes Water.

Small Water, rightly named, lies between Harter fell and High Street; and is passed by a mountain track leading from Kentmere to Mardale, over the hause called Nan Bield.——Blea Water, separated from the last by a projection of High Street, lies at the foot of a lofty rock called Blea Water Crag. Before reaching the valley, their two streams become united, and passing Mardale Green, it makes the principal feeder of Hawes Water.

*Tarns in the Feeders of Coniston Water.*

Two or three pools, between the hills on the north of Coniston Waterhead, are called simply the Tarns; while those in the western quarter have received the more dignified appellation of Waters. ——Levers Water, the largest, is situated in a wide valley, between the mountains Old Man and Wetherlam.——Low Water, placed on the Old Man's side, belies its name, as it occupies the highest level. Their united streams, after a succession of pretty waterfalls, pass Coniston Church, in their way to the lake.——Gates Water [Goat's Water,] reposes between the Old Man's western side, and the foot of the precipitous Dow Crag, [Dove Crag.] Besides being, in common with the other tarns, stocked with trout, it also contains some char. Its stream forms the Rivulet of Torver.——Blind Tarn is a small reservoir of water without a stream.——Beacon Tarn, a small one, near the foot of the lake.

Seathwaite Tarn empties itself into the river Duddon; it is separated from Levers Water, only by a narrow mountain ridge.

In the rise of the river Kent, the mere, or tarn, giving to the valley in which it was situated the name of Kentmere, has been recently annihilated in the progress of agricultural improvement. Skeggles Water, on the heath clad mountain between that and Longsleddale, is small and uninteresting.

*Tarns tributary to Derwent Lake.*

A second Blea Tarn, containing excellent trout, is situated on the heathy mountain between Wythburn and Borrowdale. After a course of nearly two miles, the water is received by Watendlath[*] Tarn, which covers about a dozen acres; but nearly destitute of fish of any kind: the trout, for which it was once famous, have been destroyed by the introduction of their enemies, the pike; yet, on account of its romantic scenery, the valley of Watendlath is still worthy of being visited. It is the stream from these tarns which, after running two miles further, along a narrow valley, forms the famed cataract of Lowdore.——Angle Tarn, stocked only with a few perch, lies on the north of Bowfell, in the head of the stream falling into the

---

[*] A specimen of the diversity of local orthography:—

*Watendlath*—Donald, 1774.
*Wattendleth*—Clarke, 1789.
*Watanlath*—West, 1796.
*Watenlath*—Hist. Cumb. 1794. Wordsworth, Green, Parson and White, Gilpin, Housman.
*Watendleth*—Ware, 1808.
*Watinlath*—Alison, 1835. Wilkinson.

branch of Borrowdale, called Langstreth. At the foot of Eagle Crag, this is joined by another stream, from the branch of Greenup; and after passing Stonethwaite and Rosthwaite, joins the Seathwaite branch a little further down the vale. ——Sprinkling Tarn, of irregular shape, reposes under Great End Crag: it abounds with excellent trout; but they are too well fed, or too wary, to be easily tempted by the bait of the angler.—— Sty-head Tarn, in some maps called Sparkling Tarn, lies about three quarters of a mile below the last, near the road to Wasdale. The water, which it receives from Sprinkling Tarn, seems to have been deprived of its nutritive qualities; as its fish are of a very inferior kind. The stream, running from thence towards Seathwaite, has some fine frothy breaks, and one grand waterfall, before it reaches the bottom of the vale.——Deck Tarn and Tarn of Leaves, one on the east side of Stonethwaite, the other between Seathwaite and Langstreth, are barely entitled to be mentioned.

Harrop Tarn, though but a small piece of water, is the principal one belonging to *Thirlmere*. It lies on the western side of Wythburn, and its stream, called Dob Gill, passing a few houses, joins the rivulet in the vale a little before it reaches the lake.

Scales Tarn, on the east end of the mountain Saddleback, is an oval piece of water, covering an area of three acres and a half, its two diameters being 176 and 124 yards, its depth 18 feet; it is uninhabited by the finny tribe. Some very exaggerated descriptions of this tarn have found their way into the History of Cumberland and other publications. From its gloomy appearance, occasioned by being overshadowed by steep rocks, its depth was supposed to be very great; and it has been represented as the crater of an extinct volcano; an assumption not supported by present appearances. Its stream, nearly encompassing Souterfell, is called the Glenderamakin, which, passing Threlkeld, joins that from Thirlmere to form the Greta.

Bowscale Tarn, which empties itself into the Caldew, is seated in a basin, singularly scooped out in the side of a hill.——Over Water lies to the north of Skiddaw, in the rise of the river Ellen.——Burtness Tarn, or Bleaberry Tarn, lies on the south-west side of Buttermere, in a recess between High Stile and Red Pike; its stream forms the cataract called Sour-milk gill.——Floutern Tarn serves as a land-mark in passing between Buttermere and Ennerdale; as Burnmoor Tarn does between Wasdale-head and Eskdale.——Devoke Water, connected with the Esk near Ravenglass, is famous for the excellence of its trout, and as a place of resort for water fowl.

There are some other small tarns, of little consequence in themselves, and seldom seen by strangers; therefore they scarcely require to be noticed. Such as Eel Tarn, Stony Tarn, and Blea Tarn, in Eskdale; Greendale Tarn, and the two Tarns above Bowderdale, in the Wasdale mountains.

LOWDORE.

## THE WATERFALLS.

Lowdore Cascade constitutes one of the most magnificent scenes of its kind among the lakes. It is not a perpendicular fall, but a foaming cataract; the water rushing impetuously from a height of 360 feet, and bounding over and among the large blocks of stone with which the channel is filled; so that when the river is full, it is a striking object at three miles distance. To the left, the perpendicular Gowder Crag, nearly five hundred feet high, towers proudly pre-eminent; while from the fissures of Shepherd's Crag on the right, the oak, ash, birch, holly, and wild rose, hang in wanton luxuriance. At the place where it is usually seen, more than half the height of the fall lies beyond the limits of the view, and in dry seasons there is a deficiency of water; yet its splendid accompaniments of wood and rock render it at all times an object deserving the notice of tourists.

Winding round Shepherd's Crag towards the top of the fall, and looking, between two finely wooded side screens, through the chasm in which the water is precipitated, a part of Derwent lake with its islands, beyond it the vale of Keswick, ornamented with white buildings, and the whole surmounted by the lofty Skiddaw—forms a picture in its kind scarcely to be equalled.

BARROW CASCADE, two miles from Keswick, has an upper and lower fall, more perpendicular than that of Lowdore, and exhibits to advantage a smaller quantity of water. From the top of the fall, the lake and vale, when not intercepted by trees, are seen in fine perspective.

WHITE WATER DASH, on the north of Skiddaw, is conspicuous from the road between Ireby and Bassenthwaite; and viewed from its foot, with the lofty Dead Crag on the right, is a good picture.

SCALE FORCE, near Buttermere, is the deepest in all the region of the lakes: it is said to fall at once one hundred and fifty-two feet, besides a smaller fall below. The water is precipitated into a tremendous chasm, between two mural rocks of sienite, beautifully overhung with trees which have fixed their roots in the crevices; the sides clad with a profusion of plants which glitter with the spray of the fall. Visitors generally scramble past the lower fall and proceed along this chasm, where the air, filled with moisture and shaded from the sun, feels cool and damp as in a cellar; till the more copious sprinkling of the spray compels them to retrace their steps.

AIREY FORCE, on Ullswater, is concealed by ancient trees, in a deep glen in Gowbarrow Park. The water, compressed between two cheeks of rock, rushes forth with great violence, and dashing from rock to rock, forms a spray, which, with the sun in a favourable direction, exhibits all the colours of the rainbow.

SKELWITH FORCE is not of great height, but it has the most copious supply of water of any cascade among the lakes. From Skelwith Bridge there is a road on the Westmorland side of the river, whence looking down upon the basin, the turmoil of the water appears very interesting; and just beyond this, there is a good view of Elterwater: but, as a picture, the fall is better seen from the Lancashire

E

side, where the Langdale Pikes, appearing between the cheeks of the rock, make an excellent distance.

RYDAL WATERFALLS.—The upper is a considerable cascade, pouring out its water, first in a contracted stream, down a perpendicular rock; and then, in a broader sheet, dashing into a deep, stony channel. The lower, being near the house, forms a beautiful garden scene.

STOCK GILL FORCE, at Ambleside, is a continuation of four falls in one; it falls from a height of 70 feet; the water, divided into two streams, after a moment's rest in the middle of the rock, is finally precipitated into the deep, shaded channel below.

HEAD OF STOCK GILL.

DUNGEON GILL is a stream issuing between the two Pikes of Langdale. The water falls about 20 yards into an awful chasm, with overhanging sides of rock, between which a large block of stone is impended like the key-stone of an arch.

COLWITH FORCE is a fine waterfall; and is but little out of the way, for those who make the tour through Little Langdale.

BIRKER FORCE, on the south side of Eskdale, is a stream of water emitted between lofty rocks, and pouring from a great elevation down the hill side in a stripe of foam.

DALEGARTH FORCE, or STANLEY GILL, on the same side of the valley, is a sublime piece of scenery. From the ancient mansion of Dalegarth Hall, now a farm house, a path has been formed, crossing the stream from side to side, three times, by lofty wooden bridges. The water falls, in successive cascades, over granite rocks, which rise on each side to a stupendous height, and are finely ornamented with trees, and fringed with a profusion of bilberry, and other plants, rooted in the crevices.

TAYLOR GILL is a dry chasm, meeting the stream of water from Sty-head Tarn near the head of the Seathwaite branch of Borrowdale; and below their junction is a lofty waterfall: a good object from the road to Wasdale.

SOUR-MILK GILL is a name applied to some mountain torrents, on account of their frothy whiteness resembling butter-milk from the churn. We have Sour-milk Gill near Buttermere, Sour-milk Gill in Grasmere, and Sour-milk Gill near the Black-lead Mine in Borrowdale.

The above enumerated are some of the most noted of the falls: but tracing the mountain streams into their deep recesses, they present an inexhaustible variety: smaller indeed, but frequently of very interesting features.

## THE RIVERS

Of this district are not of large dimensions; but issuing from rocky mountains, and running in pebbly channels, the water they contain is remarkable for its clearness and purity. From the central cluster of mountains about Bowfell, Scawfell, and Gable, many of them derive their origin; others have their source in the neighbourhood of Helvellyn and High Street.

The *Derwent* has its rise in Borrowdale; its branches are known by different names till it reaches the lake, from whence it is called the Derwent till it enters the sea.

The river issuing from Thirlmere, commonly
called St. John's beck, has formerly been called
the *Bure;* the one from Mungrisdale by Threlkeld *Glenderamakin;* after their junction it takes
the name of *Greta,* and receives the *Glenderaterra*
from between Skiddaw and Saddleback; passing
Keswick, it joins the Derwent, shortly after that
river leaves the lake. In heavy rains the Greta
sometimes rises so suddenly that it inverts the
stream of the Derwent above their junction, so
that the lake is for a short time literally filled from
all quarters. The water issuing from Buttermere,
Crummock, and Lowes Water, forms the river
*Cocker,* which falls into the Derwent at the town
named, from this circumstance, Cockermouth.
The *Ellen* rises in the mountains north of Skiddaw, and passing Uldale, Ireby, and Ellenborough,
falls into the sea at Maryport.

The several becks of Patterdale unite in Ullswater, the river issuing from thence is called the
*Eamont;* it receives the *Lowther,* from Hawes
Water, Swindale, and Wetsleddale, near Brougham
Castle; and is afterwards absorbed in the *Eden,*
which enters the Solway Frith a little below Carlisle; having first received the *Petterill,* which
rises near Greystoke, and the *Caldew,* from the
east side of Skiddaw.

Two small streams, crossing the road between
Kendal and Shap, fall into the Lune—which at
Kirkby Lonsdale is a fine river, and crossed by a

lofty antique bridge; it is navigable at Lancaster, a little below which place it falls into the sea.

The *Kent*, rising in Kentmere, receives the *Sprint* from Longsleddale, and the *Mint* from Bannisdale. It washes the skirts of Kendal, and enters the sea near Milnthrop, where it is joined by the *Belo*.

The becks of Great and Little Langdale, combined in *Ellerwater*, form the *Brathay*, and those of Grasmere and Rydal the *Rothay*, which unite in Windermere: after leaving the lake, it is called the *Leven*, which joins the *Crake* from Coniston upon the sands below Penny Bridge.

The *Duddon* rises on the south of Bowfell, and separates Cumberland from Lancashire. Unretarded by any lake, it pursues its course in a pretty transparent stream, and enters the sea on the north of the Isle of Walney.

The *Esk*, rising on the east of Scawfell, retains its name till it enters the sea at Ravenglass; where the *Irt* from Wasdale, and the *Mite* from Miterdale, join it upon the sands. The *Bleng*, passing Gosforth, falls into the Irt above Santon Bridge.

The water flowing from the north side of Gable runs in a long meandering stream down Ennerdale; it is called the *Lisa* till it enters the lake; afterwards it is the *Ehen* till it falls into the sea, half way between Ravenglass and St. Bees.——The *Calder* enters the sea near the same place.

## THE MOUNTAINS

Of the Lake district are of sufficient elevation to
command extensive prospects over the surrounding
country; yet not so high as to create any disagreeable sensations in climbing their slopes, or tra-
versing their ridges, in favourable weather.

Their magnitude imparts a sublimity to the
scenery, without overcharging the picture with any
disproportionate objects. The rocks and ravines on
their sides convey some knowledge of the materials
whereof they are composed; and, by their variety
of soil and elevation of surface, they are adapted
to the production of different kinds of vegetables.

In the summer season the bottoms of the glens
are grazed by cattle; the flocks ascend their steeps,
and nibble a scanty sustenance from the blades of
grass peeping out between the stones on the highest summits. Some of the sheep are annually
drawn from the flock, and placed in the inclosures
to fatten—and they make excellent mutton; but
many remain upon the commons during winter,
when, in deep snows, the occupation of the shepherd becomes arduous.

Foxes breed in caverns on the mountains; but
being accused of the destruction of young lambs
and poultry, the shepherds declare war against
them whenever they are found. A few Red Deer
are still remaining upon the Fells of Martindale.

Eagles, which half a century ago were frequently

seen in their lofty flights over these mountains, are
not now to be met with.   Though they built their
nests in the most inaccessible rocks, the shepherds
were so bent upon their destruction, that they con-
trived, by the help of ropes, annually to take away
or destroy either the eggs or the young; till at
length the species has been wholly exterminated
from the country.

A small bird called the Dotterel is found upon
Skiddaw, and other high mountains.  Grouse breed
in parts thickly covered with heath.   About the
latter end of October, Woodcocks begin to arrive,
and are frequently met with on the woods and
commons bordering on some of the lakes.

## SKIDDAW.

A view of the country, from at least one of the
eminent mountains of the district, is considered as
forming a part of the tour, by those who can mus-
ter strength and resolution for the undertaking;
and for this purpose Skiddaw is, on several ac-
counts, generally selected.  It is nearest to the
station at Keswick, most easy of access, as ladies
may ride on horseback to the very summit; and
standing in some measure detached, the view,
especially to the north and west, is less intercepted
by other mountains.

Skiddaw is the supreme of a group of mountains
about thirty miles in circumference; including
Saddleback, Carrock, and the Caldbeck fells: its

SKIDDAW, AND SADDLEBACK FORMERLY BLENCATHERA:—

AS SEEN ON ENTERING KESWICK FROM THE SOUTH.

WITH ANCIENT NAMES.

...The Dod

...Hullock
...Long Side
...Carlside
...Carsleddam (line 2)

...Broad End, near the
   highest point

...Skiddaw Man
...Little Man

..Howgill Tongue (line 2)

...Jenkin Hill

...Lonscale Fell

...Latrigg

...High Row Fell

...Priest Man

...Linthwaite Pike, Sad-
   dleback

...Knot Aller

...Scales Fell

height, according to Colonel Mudge, is 3022 feet above the sea. A mean of seven different trials with the barometer, between the years 1804 and the present time, makes it 2508 feet above Derwent lake; and the result of a geometrical process by the late Mr. Greatorex, in 1817, agrees with the same very nearly.

The body of the mountain is a rock of dark coloured clay-slate, in some parts of which crystals of *chyastolite* are found imbedded; and among its vegetable productions are the different species of *Lycopodium* and *Vaccinium*, the *Calluna vulgaris*, and *Empetrum nigrum*; and upon the summit the *Salix herbacea* peeps forth among the stones.

The desire of an extensive prospect being the principal motive for ascending a mountain, it is a question frequently asked, " Which is the best time of day for going up Skiddaw?" It is not easy to give a precise answer to this question; the morning is commonly recommended, and generally, the sooner you are there after the sun has fairly illumined the mountains the better; whether in an early morning, or on a dispersion of the clouds in any other part of the day.

During a clear cold night, the vapour is copiously precipitated from the higher into the lower parts of the atmosphere; so that very early in a morning, the summits of the mountains, gilded by the sun, appear in great magnificence; and the contrast of light and shade upon their sides is very interesting. But, at such times, a haziness often prevails in the valleys; which, as the air becomes warmed by the sun, again ascends; and at the same time receives an augmentation by the vapour arising from the ground; the tremulous motion of which may sometimes be perceived, as it exudes from the surface of the earth in places exposed to the most direct action of the solar rays.

After a succession of dry and hot days the air is seldom favourable for a prospect; but between showers, or when clouds prevail—provided they are above the altitude of the mountains—the view is often extended to a great distance. When the atmosphere is loaded with clouds, the middle of the day affords the greatest probability of their rising above the mountains; and a mid-day light gives the most general illumination to objects on every point of the horizon. A declining sun may throw a beautiful blaze of light upon some parts of the landscape; but its effects will not be so general; and a person remaining upon the mountain till the sun goes down, especially in Autumn, will find night come on apace as he descends.

Sometimes, when clouds have formed below the summit, the country, as viewed from above, resembles a sea of mist; a few of the highest mountain peaks having the appearance of islands, on which the sun seems to shine with unusual splendour. And when the spectator is so situated that his shadow falls upon the cloud, he may observe some curious meteorological phenomena. To those who have frequently beheld it under other circumstances, this may be a new and interesting spectacle; but a tourist, making his first and perhaps only visit, will naturally wish to have the features of the country more completely developed.

It is a grievous, though not an uncommon circumstance, to be wrapt in a cloud, which seems to be continually passing on, yet never leaves the mountain during the time appropriated for the stay; but those who are fortunate enough to be upon the summit at the very time of the cloud's departure, will experience a gratification of no common kind; when—like the rising of the curtain in a theatre—the country in a moment bursts upon the eye.

It will always be better to seize on a favourable opportunity for a mountain excursion, than to attempt to fix the time beforehand; other journeys where the state of the air is of less importance, may be deferred. A telescope may assist in the examination or recognition of a particular building or object; but in viewing the great features of the prospect it can render little assistance; it is only when the air is clear that it can be used with advantage; and then, the field of vision is so extensive, and the objects so numerous, that sufficient time is seldom afforded for individual contemplation.

From Keswick to the top of Skiddaw the barometer falls very nearly three inches; and the air often feels colder than the thermometer would seem to indicate; which may be owing, partly to the heat acquired by the exertion in climbing, and

partly to the greater quantity of moisture in the
air, with a current prevailing upon the summit; by
which the heat evolved by the body is more rapidly
dispelled from the clothing; but the difficulty of
breathing, which some have apprehended from the
diminished pressure of the atmosphere, is not
found by experience.

The distance to be travelled from Keswick to
the top of Skiddaw is nearly six miles. Since the
inclosure of the common took place, in 1810, the
way has been varied at the discretion of the gentlemen through whose grounds it lies. Visitors
have sometimes been directed to set out by the
Cockermouth road, through the toll bar; but at
present they take the Penrith turnpike, by the
side of the river Greta for half a mile; still winding
along the skirts of Latrigg, by an occupation road,
at a pleasant elevation; where the lake of Derwentwater, the town of Keswick, the beautiful
valley, and encircling mountains, are seen to great
advantage. Part of the lake of Bassenthwaite
also comes in view: but it adds little to the value
of the prospect.

Beyond the precincts of Latrigg we have little
appearance of a road; but having turned to the
right from one gate, and to the left from the next,
a wall—first on the left hand, and afterwards on
the right—points out the way. The ascent hitherto
has been so gentle, that at the distance of three
miles we have reached but one third of the required
altitude: but now we begin to encounter a more

steep part of the mountain. As we advance in
height, the objects in the valley appear to be
diminished in magnitude and importance; but our
prospects are enlarged, by mountains at a greater
distance rising into view; among which are those
of Coniston, and the hyperbolic summit of the
Pike of Stickle, in Langdale.

Having reached one half of the altitude, the
wall makes a turn to the right, where we leave it
—our path lying more directly up the hill—and
having combated this steep for about a quarter of
a mile further, we find ourselves upon a turfy plain
of moderate acclivity; and by degrees obtain a
view of the sea, with a portion of Scotland beyond
it—the Isle of Man gradually advancing from behind the western mountains. In a small hollow,
if the weather is not too droughty, we meet with
a spring of water; and, as it is the last by the way,
it may be taken advantage of to dilute the brandy,
which—with a few biscuits or sandwiches—a pro-
vident guide will not forget to recommend.

We are now upon the verge of a tract bearing
the name of Skiddaw Forest, although without a
tree. The heath is well stocked with grouse, for
the protection of which a lodge was erected by the
late Earl of Egremont. Here the river Caldew
takes its rise; and from hence in a serpentine
course makes its way to Carlisle. A new view to
the northward now opens to us, over the narrow
part of Solway Frith, into Scotland; and we descry
the long-looked-for pile upon the summit of the

r

mountain. Following a beaten track, we leave a
double-pointed hill on our left, beyond which succeeds another steep ascent of 500 feet, where we
suddenly regain a view of Derwentwater and the
mountains beyond it. At the top of this steep we
reach the last point seen from the valley; it is the
south end of a ridge, covered with fragments of
slaty rock ; and towards its further end lies the
object of our journey, which is marked by a large
pile of stones, erected in 1826, by a detachment of
the Ordnance surveyors. Here the lake of Derwent and vale of Keswick are hid from us; but our
attention is now arrested by more distant objects.

The town of Whitehaven is concealed from our
sight; but the headlands of St. Bees beyond it are
conspicuous; and the Isle of Man in the same
direction. Workington, with its shipping, may
be seen due west, and further northwards Maryport, and the fashionable bathing place of Allonby.
Cockermouth, with its church and castle, is seen
over the foot of Bassenthwaite Lake; and between
us and the borders of Scotland lies a large extent
of cultivated country, in which the city of Carlisle
stands as a central object. Beyond Solway Frith,
the mountain Criffel, in Kircudbrightshire, appears
near the shore; and on its right is the mouth of
the river Nith, on which stands the town of Dum-
fries. To the left lies the small island called
Hasten, at the foot of the water of Orr; and further west, the mouth of the Dee, at Kirkcudbright,
opening into the large bay of Wigton. Beyond

it, the bay of Glenluce, with Burrow Head, and
the Mull of Galloway, are sometimes visible.
The houses and cornfields on the Scottish coast
are often distinguishable; with mountains rising
behind mountains to an interminable distance.
The Cheviot hills appear in the direction of High
Pike; but it would be in vain to look for the
German Ocean, which has sometimes been represented as visible from hence.

Penrith and its Beacon may be seen, and beyond
it the lofty Crossfell, with some of the eminences
bordering upon Northumberland, Durham, and
Yorkshire.    To the right of Penrith are the walls
of Brougham Castle, and the mansion of Lord
Brougham   The hills surrounding Ullswater are
in view; and the top of Ingleborough appears
beyond the end of High Street.  Through the
gap of Dunmail Raise, the estuary of the Kent,
below Milnthorp, appears in two small portions,
separated by the intervention of Yewbarrow, a
hill in Witherslack; and the castle of Lancaster
may sometimes be discerned with a telescope,
beyond the southern edge of Gummers-how, in
Cartmel Fells.

The superior eminences of Scawfell and Gable
have been in full view during our ascent, and we
may now discover Black Comb through an opening between the latter and Kirkfell; and part of
the Screes mountain beyond Wast Water, between
Kirkfell and the Pillar.  In the same direction,
may Snowdon, in Wales, possibly be sometimes

discerned; and to the right of the Isle of Man, perhaps the Irish mountains; but ninety-nine times out of a hundred it would be in vain to look for either.

It would be superfluous to enumerate more of the objects which on a very fine day may be seen from this mountain; it is the province of the guide to point them out as they rise into view, or as a favourable light renders them most clearly discernable. It is not those objects that are seldom and dimly seen, that ought to receive the greatest attention; but rather such as may be distinctly known and properly appreciated. It must not be expected that objects at fifty miles distance should appear as distinct as those near at hand; indeed it often happens, that they cannot be seen at all, though the air to a moderate distance seems remarkably clear; yet still a person who sets out with a disposition to be pleased, will, on any tolerably fine day, be sufficiently compensated for his trouble; and the more the distant objects are veiled from view, the higher will the near ones rise in estimation.

One of the most vexatious circumstances, and which not unfrequently happens, is to meet with a small cap of cloud upon the summit, that entirely excludes all prospect from thence; in such a case, the party—if on foot, and not over timid—ought to be conducted from the south end of the ridge downwards about 600 feet to a part of the mountain called Carlside, where most of the objects

may be seen that should have been visible from the
summit, and the homeward journey, by the hamlet
of Millbeck, not at all lengthened—only in parts
steeper. By deviating from Carlside tarn, along
the ridge to the point of Hullock, the city of
Carlisle may just be seen; and an unrivalled view
of Bassenthwaite Lake. A party on horseback
might go a little to the northward from the summit, make their descent into the valley of Bassenthwaite, and after refreshing at the Castle
Inn, return to Keswick on the western side of the
Lake.

## HELVELLYN

Affords a more complete geographical display of
the lake district than any other point within its
limits: several of the lakes may be viewed from
thence, and the mountains in every direction appear in a most splendid arrangement; while, from
the south to the western part of the horizon, the
distant ocean may be discerned through several of
the spaces between them.

According to Colonel Mudge, the height of
Helvellyn above the level of the sea is 3055 feet.
It is about 2540 feet above the Nag's Head, at
Wythburn, from which place it is most frequently
ascended; the distance here being the shortest,
and a guide can be had. It is too steep to make
use of horses; but by an active person on foot it
is easily surmountable. The ascent on this side is

no where difficult or dangerous; it may be commenced at the six mile stone, at the King's Head,
or other places nearer Keswick, where the views
in the progress upwards are less circumscribed
than at Wythburn. By leaving the turnpike road
at Fisher Place, the waterfalls in Brotto Gill on
the left hand are brought into notice; in one of
these the water is projected further from the rock
than in any other cascade in the neighbourhood.
From this place, as we advance in altitude, the
lakes of Thirlmere and Bassenthwaite are gradually developed to the sight; Skiddaw and Saddleback being in view to the north; and the
mountains lying to the south-west progressively
appearing to rise up beyond the long and uninteresting fell, which lies between the lake of Thirlmere and the valley of Borrowdale.

On the western side of the mountain, about the
distance of three hundred yards from its summit,
and three hundred perpendicular feet below it,
there is a spring called Brownrigg Well, where
the water issues in all seasons in a copious stream;
its temperature in the summer months being generally from 40° to 42°; and when mixed with a
little brandy, as recommended by "mine host" of
the Nag's Head, it makes a grateful beverage.

This mountain is also frequently ascended from
Patterdale; where, for three-fourths of the way, the
ascent is gentle, and gradually opens out pleasing
views of the lake of Ullswater, with the scenery
around and beyond it. More immediately below,

is the narrow vale of Grisedale, surmounted by the
lofty St. Sunday Crag, which casts its solemn shade
into the valley. On reaching the first ridge of the
mountain, the long-looked-for summit pile is discovered on the top of a rocky precipice, seven
hundred feet in height above Red Tarn, which
lies enclosed in the bosom of the mountain before
us. From hence the shortest way is one that
many would hesitate to venture upon; while others
might think it a stigma upon their courage to de-
cline it. It lies along the top of Striding Edge,
which in some parts affords little more footing than
the ridge of a house, while its sides are far steeper
than an ordinary roof. A less difficult way is to
leave the tarn on the left hand, ascending Swirrel
Edge, which is comparatively smooth; yet here is
a little rocky scrambling to gain the top of the
precipice; in the midst of which it will be well to
halt, and take a view of Bassenthwaite Lake with
its environs; which cannot be seen from the highest part of the mountain.

The ground towards the summit forms a kind of
moss-clad plain, sloping gently to the west, and
terminated on the east by a series of rocky precipices; and here the prospect on every side is grand
beyond conception. Considerable portions of the
lakes of Ullswater, Windermere, Coniston, and
Esthwaite, with several of the mountain tarns, are
to be seen. Red Tarn is seated so deeply below the
eye, that, compared with its gigantic accompaniments, it would scarcely be estimated at more than

half its actual dimensions. To the right and left of Red Tarn, the two narrow ridges called Striding Edge and Swirrel Edge, are stretched out in the direction of the lamina of the slaty rock, of which this part of the mountain is composed. Beyond Swirrel Edge lies Keppel-cove Tarn; and at the termination of the ridge rises the peak of Catsty-cam, modernized into Catchedecam, or Catchety-cam. Angle Tarn, and the frothy stream from Ayes Water, may be seen among the hills beyond Patterdale; and more remote, the estuaries of the Kent and Leven, uniting in the wide bay of Morecambe, and extending to the distant ocean. Chapel Isle is an object in the Ulverston channel; and a small triangular piece of water, near the middle of Windermere, serves as a direction to the town and Castle of Lancaster, which are sometimes visible from hence. The sea, circumscribing the western half of the Lake district, from Lancaster sands to the Solway Frith, is here and there visible between the peaks of the distant mountains; each portion in succession reflecting the sun's rays to the eye of the spectator, as the luminary descends towards the western horizon.

On the banks of Ullswater, Hallsteads, the beautiful summer retreat of John Marshall, Esq., occupies a prominent station. From the foot of the lake the vale of Eamont leads towards Brougham-Hall and the ruins of the ancient Castle near it. The cultivated country about Penrith is bounded by a chain of mountains topped by the lofty Cross-

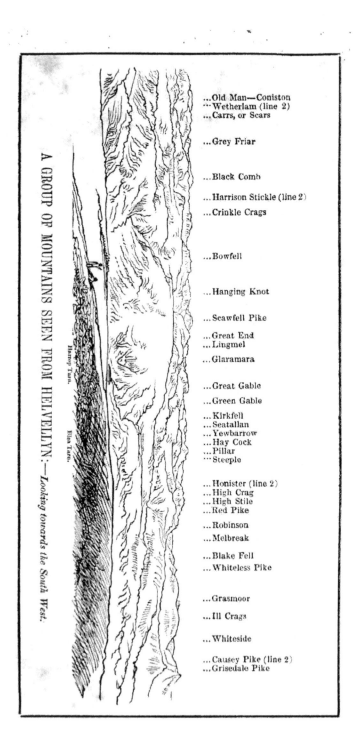

A GROUP OF MOUNTAINS SEEN FROM HELVELLYN:— *Looking towards the South West.*

Harrop Tarn.

Eliza Tarn.

...Old Man—Coniston
···Wetherlam (line 2)
...Carrs, or Scars

...Grey Friar

...Black Comb

...Harrison Stickle (line 2)

...Crinkle Crags

...Bowfell

...Hanging Knot

...Scawfell Pike

...Great End
...Lingmel

...Glaramara

...Great Gable

...Green Gable

...Kirkfell
...Seatallan
...Yewbarrow
...Hay Cock
...Pillar
···Steeple

...Honister (line 2)
...High Crag
...High Stile
...Red Pike

...Robinson

...Melbreak

...Blake Fell
...Whiteless Pike

...Grasmoor

...Ill Crags

...Whiteside

...Causey Pike (line 2)
...Grisedale Pike

fell; to the right of which are high grounds separating Westmorland from Durham and Yorkshire;
and further still to the right, the crowned head of
Ingleborough stands conspicuous. Black Comb,
in the distance beyond Wrynose, fills up the space
between the fells of Coniston and Langdale;
Crinkle Crags and Bowfell are exceeded in altitude
by the Pikes on Scawfell; and on the opposite
side of Sty-head, the Gable rears his head to a
considerable elevation. The Isle of Man appears
to be raised up to the top of Kirkfell, the distance
of more than fifty miles between them being overlooked.

The Pillar of Ennerdale holds a respectable
station; and the mountain beyond Buttermere,
with its three protuberances, High Crag, High
Stile, and Red Pike, rises behind Honister Crag
and the Dalehead of Newlands. Grasmoor and
Grisedale Pike look well up among their neighbours, while Skiddaw and Saddleback abate nothing of their importance on being viewed from
this elevation. The mountains of Scotland, seen
beyond the Solway Frith, fill up the distance; and
nearer to our station, High Street, Ill-bell, Fairfield, and many other neighbouring eminences,
ought not to be overlooked. Place Fell, and
other mountains of Martindale, rise boldly beyond
Ullswater; but between this and the foot of Hawes
Water, they present less variety of outline.

By travelling along the ridge, to a little distance
each way, a variety of prospects may be enjoyed;
which those who return directly leave unseen. On

proceeding a little northward, one of the islands on Windermere comes in view; and at the lower or northern man, the lakes of Thirlmere and Bassenthwaite; by deviating a little to the westward, we see a small portion of Grasmere; and by following the edge of the precipice from the summit to some distance southward, better views of Patterdale present themselves; and the descent to Wythburn may then be made, down steeply sloping ground, to a rocky knoll called Bursett Crag; where is a good view of Thirlmere, as also of Bassenthwaite Lake. Such as wish to descend at Grasmere may go southwards to the foot of Grisdale Tarn, where a track will be found which joins the turnpike road five miles from Ambleside; but the best view of Grasmere will be had by leaving the tarn on the left, and proceeding over Seat Sandal.

Some have extended their excursion from Helvellyn to Fairfield, holding on the mountain ridge to Ambleside; but after making the unavoidable descent of 1350 feet to Grisedale Tarn, a second ascent of 1230 feet will mostly be thought too fatiguing. By exertion too long continued, the mind as well as the body becomes enervated, and incapable of enjoyment; as it has been known in some, who, travelling through Borrowdale in a morning, would not overlook the most trifling object; yet, in the latter part of the same day, have passed the most interesting scenes on Wast Water, without making any other inquiry than, "How far is it to the inn?"

## SCAWFELL AND THE PIKES.

Scawfell is the name that has generally been given, in maps, to the mountain connecting the heads of Borrowdale, Eskdale, and Wasdale. It is the highest ground in all this mountainous district, and indeed in that part of the united kingdom called England. The several lofty peaks by which it is distinguished are known in the neighbourhood by different names. The two most eminent are stated, by Colonel Mudge, to be 3166 and 3092 feet in height. I have estimated their difference at 60 feet; which, from various observations made between the two points, I am convinced is rather in excess than otherwise. Rising from one of the lowest vallies, the highest point is 3000 feet above Wast Water.

The lower of these points, lying to the south-west, is a bulky mountain—the proper Scawfell; the higher, rising from a narrower base, has been called the Pikes. For want of a designation sufficiently explicit, strangers have sometimes been mistakenly directed to the secondary point; and to cross the deep chasm of Mickle Door, by which they are separated, is a work of considerable difficulty; although the direct distance does not exceed three quarters of a mile. Latterly, however, it seems, by common consent, the highest point is called Scawfell Pikes; and since the erection of the large pile and staff upon it, in 1826, there is no danger of mistaking the place.

Excepting some tufts of moss, very little vegetation is to be seen upon these summits. They are chiefly composed of rocks, and large blocks of stone piled one upon another; and their weather-worn surfaces prove that they have long remained in their present state. The prevailing rock is a kind of indurated slate, in layers of finer and coarser materials, which gives to the surface a ribbed or furrowed appearance; the finer parts are compact and hard as flint: and here the *lichen geographicus* appears in peculiar beauty.

Scawfell-Pikes may be ascended on foot from any of the adjacent vales, but most conveniently from Borrowdale; yet the distance from a place of entertainment, the ruggedness of the ground, and the danger of being caught in a cloud—to which, from its situation, it is more subject than its neighbours—altogether conspire against its being visited by any other than hardy pedestrians: and strangers should so calculate their time, that night may not overtake them on such places. To be enveloped in a cloud is of itself disagreeable; cloud and night together would be dreadful.

Horses and carriages may be used as far as Seathwaite, in Borrowdale, after which the mountain may be ascended on foot at the discretion of the conductor. One way is to leave the Wasdale road at the bridge, proceeding by the side of the gill towards the pass called Esk Hause, and from thence turning up the back of Great-end, which presents its bold rocky front towards Borrowdale,

and commands extensive prospects towards both
Derwentwater and Windermere. Beyond this
there are two unavoidable dips and rises before
the summit of the highest Pike can be gained.
Another way is to follow the Wasdale road to Sty-
head Tarn; from thence, with Great-end Crag
on the right, pass Sprinkling Tarn, and join the
before-mentioned route. This is perhaps the
easiest way, but rather circuitous. From Sty-
head Tarn the ascent may be made by steep clam-
bering to the top of Great-end, which affords fine
views by the way, and is nearer than the last.
But many—after having arrived at Sty-head, and
obtained a sight of the pile—will be inclined to
take the shortest way, by the foot of the great
rocks, with a steep ascent at last to the summit.
And those who take the last-mentioned route in
their progress, should be advised to pass over
Great-end and the intermediate summits in returning, for the sake of the varied prospects which
they afford.

The divergency of several vallies from this point,
has been compared to the spokes of a wheel; and
in tracing their courses upon a map, the simile
may be applicable enough; but upon the spot, the
resemblance is not so striking—the mountains run
athwart one another in such a way, that little can
be seen of the intervening vallies.

Here we overlook an immense assemblage of
mountains, exhibiting the stern grandeur of their
rocky summits; but their general arrangement is

G

not so splendid, nor their forms so stately, as when viewed from Helvellyn, or from the ascent to Skiddaw; and there is a deficiency of the rich lowland views that may be had from the latter mountain.

Satiated by mountain scenery, the eye is instinctively turned towards the sea, which opens to a great extent, and shews the various indentations of the Lancashire and Cumberland coast; with the isle of Walney stretching from the bay of Morecambe to the estuary of the Duddon. The top of Ingleborough may be seen in the distance; but it requires a very clear atmosphere to discern the mountains of North Wales, which stretch out to the right of Black Comb. The Isle of Man is frequently visible; and, when the surface of the sea is covered with a thin film of vapour, the effect at first sight is curious; the island appearing more like an object in the clouds than one seated in the water. The fells of Coniston exclude the view of Lancaster sands; but an opening, between the Old Man and Dow Crag, directs to the church and castle of Lancaster. Some portions of Scotland appear on the right and left of the Ennerdale and Derwent Fells; and we are just permitted to see a part of the lake of Windermere, between the Low Wood Inn and Bowness; also the eastern side of Derwentwater, and a part of Wast Water with Devoke Water, Sty-head Tarn, and a small mountain tarn, above Bowderdale.

From a point a little to the southward, we can take a peep into the head of the vale of Eskdale, far below us; and beyond it, see a single habitation in Seathwaite, near the rise of the Duddon. Passing towards Great-end a portion of Crummock Lake comes in sight; and from Great-end, and Esk Hause, there are more open views towards the head of Windermere, Loughrigg, Elterwater, and Derwentwater.

## SADDLEBACK

—Being at a greater distance from the station at Keswick than Skiddaw, of somewhat inferior elevation, and the ascent not quite so easy—is seldom visited by strangers. It is better situated than Skiddaw for a view towards the south, and also of the neighbourhood of Lowther and Penrith; but the western view is greatly intercepted. It has formerly been called Blencathera, and it is from its shape, as seen from the vicinity of Penrith, that it has received the name of Saddleback. Its height is 2787 feet, and its rock is a primitive clay-slate, similar to that of Skiddaw. The southern side is formed into a series of deep ravines and rocky projections; while to the north, it descends in a smooth grassy slope: and in a deep hollow, below a rocky precipice on its eastern end, a small dark tarn is curiously placed; as more fully described at page 33.

On two occasions, in 1743–4, the aerial phenomenon called *mirage* was observed on a portion of this mountain called Soutra Fell: the lover of the marvellous will find an ample detail of the circumstances in " Clarke's Survey of the Lakes."

## GABLE, OR GREAT GAVEL

—So called from its shape—is a fine object as viewed from Wasdale, from Ennerdale, or from Crummock Lake; it is also seen from Windermere. It is 2925 feet in height, and was remarkable for a well of pure water on the very summit. This was not a spring issuing in the common way out of the earth; but was supplied immediately from the atmosphere, in the shape of rains and dews. It was, till partly demolished, a triangular receptacle in the rock, six inches deep, and capable of holding about two gallons; which, by containing water in the driest seasons, served to shew how slight a degree of evaporation is carried on at this altitude. The rock of Gable is a very hard, compact, dark-coloured stone, with garnets imbedded.

## THE PILLAR

—A mountain rivalling the Gable in height—is situated between the vale of Ennerdale and that branch of Wasdale-head called Mosedale. It presents, towards Ennerdale, one of the grandest rocky fronts anywhere to be met with; and has derived its name from a projecting rock on this side, which was originally called the Pillar Stone, and had been considered as inaccessible, till an adventurous shepherd reached its summit, in 1826. The rock is a kind of greenstone, more porphyritic than that of Gable.

## BOWFELL

Rises proudly in view from Windermere and Esthwaite Lakes. It is 2911 feet in height, and sheds the rain water into Borrowdale, Langdale, and Eskdale. It is easiest of access from Langdale, but may be reached from any of the above mentioned vales, or from the vale of Duddon.

## GRASMOOR

Is a bold rocky mountain on the eastern side of Crummock Lake; it is sometimes called Grasmire, a name in no wise corresponding with its appearance. It rises to the height of 2756 feet. The side towards the lake is extremely rocky and barren; but the eastern side is a grassy slope, and on its summit is a plain of several acres. It affords a good bird's-eye view of the Lakes of Buttermere, Crummock, and Loweswater, with their adjacent mountains; and a considerable portion of the Cumberland and Scottish coasts.

## GRISEDALE PIKE

Rises to a lofty apex, as its name implies. It is 2580 feet in height; and is well situated for a view of the vale of Keswick to the east; and a considerable part of the county of Cumberland, with the sea, the Isle of Man, and the mountains of Galloway, to the west and north.

g 2

## CARROCK FELL

Makes one of the flanks of that mountain group, whereof Skiddaw forms the crown. It is upwards of 2000 feet in height; and shews a double pointed summit, on which a space appears to have been once inclosed by a wall. Its basis is a crystalline rock of the nature of sienite; and in its neighbourhood are veins of lead and copper, with other substances highly interesting to the mineralogist and geologist.

## BLACK COMB,

Pronounced Black-Coom, probably from the dark hollow on its south-east side, stands near the southern boundary of Cumberland. Forming the extremity of the mountain chain, it may be seen at a great distance; and is a fine station both for land and sea prospects. In 1808, it was made one of Colonel Mudge's stations, in the process of the Trigonometrical Survey. He calculated its height to be 1919 feet above the level of the sea. Its substance is a rock of clay-slate, similar to that of Skiddaw, covered by a large tract of peat earth, which is used for fuel in the adjacent hamlets.

## CONISTON FELL.

The highest point of Coniston Fell is called THE OLD MAN, from the pile of stones erected on its summit; which, in 1833, was rebuilt in a more substantial manner. It is 2577 feet in height, and has a good view of the rocky mountains, Scawfell and Bowfell, and, at a distance, the highest point of Skiddaw. Coniston Lake is seen in full proportion, with a part of Windermere. Two tarns appear upon the mountain, the smaller called Low Water, though on a higher level, the larger Levers Water; and on the western side of the hill, but not seen from the summit, is Gates Water, lying at the foot of the precipitous Dow Crag. Standing open to the south, unincumbered by other mountains, the Old Man commands a complete view of all the fine bays and estuaries of the Lancashire and part of the Cumberland coast—the Isles of Walney and Man—and over the mouth of the river Duddon, on a favourable day, Snowdon and its neighbouring mountains may sometimes be distinguished.

Beginning to ascend at the Black Bull, near Coniston Church, you meet on your left a stream abounding in pretty waterfalls; the copper mines near Levers Water, and slate quarries between Low Water and the summit, can be seen by the way; and the descent may be made, at choice, more in front of the mountain. Those who admire a lengthened mountain excursion, may begin the ascent at Fellfoot, in Little Langdale, and surmounting the Carrs and the Old Man, descend to Coniston.

The summit of the hill, like the quarries on its sides, is of a fine, pale blue, roofing slate. In some places a hard felspathic rock abounds; and between this and Coniston Church, on the western side of the stream, the commencement of the darker coloured slate may be observed.

## FAIRFIELD

—2950 feet above the level of the sea—makes a fine mountain excursion from Ambleside, commencing the ascent at Rydal, encircling Rydal head, and returning to Ambleside by Nook End. Lakes and Tarns to the number of ten, may be enumerated in this excursion; viz., Ullswater, Windermere, Esthwaite, Coniston, Grasmere, and Rydal lakes; and Elterwater, Blelham, Easdale, Codale, and Grisedale tarns: oftener than once, may eight of them be reckoned from one station. Here is likewise a good view of the different creeks and inlets of the sea towards Lancaster and Ulverston.

## LANGDALE PIKES,

Called PIKE OF STICKLE, and HARRISON STICKLE, are by their peculiar form distinguished at a great distance. They afford some good views to the south-east: but being encompassed on other sides by higher mountains, the prospect is somewhat limited. Harrison Stickle, the higher, is 2400 feet above the level of the sea: it is more easily ascended, and has the better prospect towards Rydal and Ambleside; but the Pike of Stickle has the advantage of catching, through an opening in the hills, a more perfect view of the lake of Bassenthwaite, and the mountain Skiddaw—from both of which Harrison Stickle is nearly excluded by the interposition of higher lands.

## HIGH STREET

Seems to have taken its name from an ancient road which appears as a broad green path over this mountain. It is probably the highest road ever formed in England, being 2700 feet above the level of the sea. On account of its central situation, between the vales of Patterdale, Martindale, Mardale, Kentmere, and Troutbeck, and being connected with others at a little distance; an annual meeting was formerly held here, when the shepherds of the several vales reciprocally communicated intelligence of such sheep as might have strayed beyond their proper bounds; and to enliven the meeting, races and other diversions were instituted; ale and cakes being supplied from the neighbouring villages. Highstreet affords some good prospects; but being at a distance from any place of entertainment, it is seldom visited by strangers. Pedestrians, fond of mountain rambles, might, with a guide, pass over it from Patterdale into Troutbeck, or Kentmere; or into Mardale, and thence by Hawes Water to Bampton—from whence are roads to Pooley Bridge, Lowther, Penrith, and Shap.

## WANSFELL PIKE

Stands near the junction of the green slate with the dark slaty limestone. It rises nearly 1500 feet above Windermere Lake. This is a moderate elevation compared with many of its neighbours; yet it is not deficient in prospects. It affords excellent views of Windermere, Grasmere, and Rydal lakes; the towns of Ambleside and Hawkshead, with the beautifully diversified scenery in the neighbourhood. Further distant are seen the sands of Milnthorp, Lancaster, and Ulverston, with the majestic mountains of Coniston and Langdale. In a walk from the pike, towards Kirkstone, it is curious to observe Great Gable start out, as it were, from behind Langdale Pikes, and appearing to separate itself from them still further as the spectator makes his progress along this ridge. Wansfell may be conveniently visited either from Ambleside or Low Wood Inn: and a walk across the Troutbeck Hundreds, from the public house, called the Mortal Man, to Skelgill, has been highly recommended.

## WHITELESS PIKE

Is attached to the mountain Grasmoor, and rises with a steep ascent to the height of nearly 2000 feet above Buttermere. It commands excellent views of the three lakes of Buttermere, Crummock, and Loweswater; with the summits of all the principal mountains from Helvellyn to those of Borrowdale, Wasdale, Ennerdale, and Buttermere. The Isle of Man is also in sight, and a considerable portion of the shires of Kirkcudbright and Wigton, in Scotland.

## LOUGHRIGG FELL

Is scarcely 1000 feet above Windermere, and 900 above Grasmere Lake, and the moderate degree of exertion required to climb it, will be amply repaid by the prospects. It is just what might be wished in the place where it stands—high enough to command a view of the circumjacent valleys; and not so lofty as to lessen the importance of the surrounding mountains. Every rocky knoll presents a new combination of scenery. Windermere, a fine expanse of water with its ornamented banks; the town of Hawkshead and its environs, with Blelham Tarn, and the irregularly shaped Esthwaite Water; Loughrigg with its Tarn, and Langdale with Elterwater; the beautiful vales of Grasmere and Rydal, with their two lakes; and the town and highly embellished neighbourhood of Ambleside are the lowland objects. The circumscribing mountains of Coniston Langdale, Grasmere, Rydal, Ambleside and Troutbeck, are at such eligible distances, that not only their elegantly formed outlines, but also their varied surface of rock and verdure, can clearly be distinguished. Small portions of Coniston Water and Thirlmere are just sufficient to shew the places of those two lakes. The mountain Skiddaw seen over Dunmail Raise, and the top of Ingleborough in the direction of the Low Wood Inn, are extraneous objects beyond the common bounds of the panorama.

## STATION I.—SCAWFELL highest point, THE PIKES.

Latitude 54° 27' 24" N.   Longitude 3° 12' W.
Height 3160 feet.

| | BEARINGS | Distances in miles. | Height in feet |
|---|---|---|---|
| Skiddaw .................................... | 10° NE | 14 | 3022 |
| Ingleborough, *Yorkshire* .................. | 58 SE | 38 | 2361 |
| Black Comb, *Cumberland* ....... ......... | 19 SW | 15 | 1919 |
| Snowdon, *Caernarvonshire* ............... | 20 SW | 103 | 3571 |
| Holyhead Mountain, *Anglesea* .......... | 37 SW | 100 | 709 |
| North Barule, *Isle of Man* .............. | 76 SW | 49 | 1804 |
| Sleiph Donard, *Ireland* .................... | 79 SW | 112 | 2820 |
| Mull of Galloway, *Scotland* .............. | 77 NW | 68 | —— |
| Burrow Head, *Scotland* .................... | 68 NW | 51 | —— |
| Crif Fell, *Scotland* ......................... | 26 NW | 38 | 1831 |

## STATION II.—SKIDDAW.

Latitude 54° 39' 12" N.   Longitude 3° 8' 9" W.
Height 3022 feet.

| | | | |
|---|---|---|---|
| Wisp Hill, *near Mospaul Inn* ........... | 9° NE | 45 | 1940 |
| Carlisle ................................... | 26 NE | 19 | —— |
| Cheviot Hill, *Northumberland* ........... | 35 NE | 70 | 2658 |
| Cross Fell, *Cumberland* ................... | 82 NE | 27 | 2901 |
| Saddleback ................................ | 78 SE | 4 | 2787 |
| Nine Standards, *Westmorland* ... ...... | 68 SE | 38 | 2136 |
| Ingleborough ............................ . | 42 SE | 46 | 2361 |
| Helvellyn ................................. | 32 SE | 10 | 3070 |
| Black Comb .............................. | 15 SW | 29 | 1919 |
| Snowdon .................................. | 19 SW | 118 | 3571 |
| Snea Fell, *Isle of Man* ................... | 64 SW | 59 | 2004 |
| Sleiph Donard, *Down* ..................... | 73 SW | 120 | 2820 |
| Bryal Point, *nearest in Ireland* ......... | 82 SW | 91 | —— |
| Mull of Galloway ...................... ... | 89 NW | 69 | —— |
| Burrow Head .............................. | 84 NW | 50 | —— |
| Crif Fell .................................. | 43 NW | 28 | 1831 |
| Ben Lomond, *Stirling* .................... | 30 NW | 120 | 3420 |
| Ben Nevis, *Inverness* .................... | 28 NW | 170 | 4358 |
| Queensberry Hill ......................... | 22 NW | 48 | 2259 |

## STATION III.—HELVELLYN.

Latitude 54° 31′ 43″ N.   Longitude 3° 0′ 21″ W.
Height 3070 feet.

| | BEARINGS | | Distances in miles | Height in feet. |
|---|---|---|---|---|
| Cheviot | 28° | NE | 75 | 2658 |
| Cross Fell | 60 | NE | 24 | 2901 |
| Stainmoor | 88 | SE | 34 | —— |
| Ingleborough | 45 | SE | 36 | 2361 |
| Bidston Lighthouse, *Cheshire* | 1 | SW | 79 | —— |
| Garreg Mountain, *Flintshire* | 8 | SW | 87 | 835 |
| Old Man, *Coniston* | 21 | SW | 12 | 2577 |
| Snowdon | 24 | SW | 112 | 3571 |
| Snea Fell | 74 | | 61 | 2004 |
| Crif Fell | 40 | NW | 38 | 1831 |

## STATION IV.—CONISTON OLD MAN.

Latitude 54° 22′ 20″ N.   Longitude 3° 6′ 34″ W.
Height 2577 feet.

| | | | | |
|---|---|---|---|---|
| Calf, *near Sedbergh* | 90° | E | 25 | 2188 |
| Great Whernside, *Kettlewell* | 72 | SE | 48 | 2263 |
| Whernside, *near Dent* | 71 | SE | 31 | 2384 |
| Pennygant | 70 | SE | 38 | 2270 |
| Ingleborough | 64 | SE | 33 | 2361 |
| Pendle Hill | 44 | SE | 49 | 1803 |
| Lancaster | 31 | SE | 25 | —— |
| Moel Fammau, *Denbigh* | 4 | SW | 85 | 1845 |
| Carnedd Llewellyn, *Caernarvon* | 23 | SW | 92 | 3469 |
| Carnedd David, *Caernarvon* | 23 | 30′ | 93 | 3427 |
| Snowdon, *Caernarvon* | 23 | 40′ | 99 | 3571 |
| Penmaen Mawr, *Caernarvon* | 24 | SW | 85 | 1540 |
| Holyhead Mountain | 41 | SW | 98 | 709 |
| Black Comb | 46 | SW | 12 | 1919 |
| Snea Fell | 84 | SW | 55 | 2004 |
| Burrow Head | 64 | NW | 56 | —— |
| Skiddaw | 4 | NW | 20 | 3022 |

[The foregoing tables include some eminent mountains beyond the limits of the map, to shew their relative positions and height; without intending to say that all of them can be discerned from the station under which they are placed.]

H

## THE CRAGS.

Some of the most remarkable Crags are—The Pillar, in Ennerdale; Honister Crag, near Buttermere; Scawfell Crags, between Wasdale Head and Eskdale; Broad Crag on the Wasdale side, and Broad Crag on the Eskdale side, of Scawfell Pikes; Paveyark, in Langdale; Rainsbarrow Crag, in Kentmere; Saint Sunday Crag, in Patterdale; Wallow Crag, near Keswick, and Wallow Crag, near Hawes Water; Wallow-barrow Crag, in the vale of Duddon; Castle Crag, in Mardale, Castle Crag, in Borrowdale (said to have been a Roman station), and Castle Head, near Keswick; Green Crag, in Legberthwaite, sometimes called the Enchanted Castle, or Castle Rock of St. John's; Gait Crag [Goat Crag], in Borrowdale, Gait Crag and Iron Crag, near Shoulthwaite, and Gait Crag, in Langdale; Dow Crag [Dove Crag], in Coniston Fells, Dove Crags, in Patterdale, and Dow Crag, in Eskdale; Bull Crag and Littledale Crag, in the vale of Newlands; Eagle Crag, in Borrowdale, Eagle Crag, in Buttermere, and Eagle Crag, in Patterdale: Falcon Crag, near Derwent Lake; and a Raven Crag in almost every vale: one of the most conspicuous of which is that overlooking Leathes Water.

———————

DRUIDICAL CIRCLE, NEAR KESWICK.

# THE ANTIQUITIES.

A Druidical Circle, 100 feet by 108 in diameter, in a field adjoining the old Penrith road, at the top of the hill, a mile and a half from Keswick. It is formed by rough *cobble* stones of various sizes, similar to what are scattered over the surface, and imbedded in the diluvium of the adjacent grounds. The largest stands upwards of seven feet in height, and may weigh about eight tons.

LONG MEG AND HER DAUGHTERS.

A monument of the same kind, but of far larger dimensions, called Long Meg and her Daughters, stands near Little Salkeld, seven miles N. E. of Penrith. This circle is 350 paces in circumference, and is composed of 67 massy unformed stones, many of them 10 feet in height. At seventeen paces from the southern side of the circle, stands Long Meg—a square unhewn column of red freestone, nearly 15 feet in girth, and 18 feet high.

On the common called Burnbanks, near the foot of Hawes water, there are five tumuli of earth, called Giants' Graves.

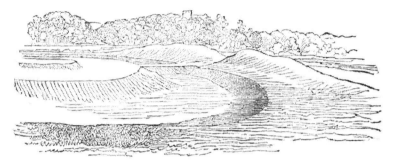

KING ARTHUR'S ROUND TABLE.

"——— Red Penrith's TABLE ROUND,
For feats of chivalry renown'd."—SIR W. SCOTT.

King Arthur's Round Table is a circular plot of ground about 52 yards in diameter, encompassed by a trench and bank of earth; with places of entrance on two opposite sides. It is situated between the rivers Eamont and Lowther, rather more than a mile from Penrith, in an angle between the road to Kendal and that to Pooley Bridge.

Mayburgh lies about a quarter of a mile distant from the last, between the river Eamont and the road to Pooley. An area of near one hundred yards in diameter is circumscribed by a mound, formed of an enormous quantity of pebble stones, apparently gathered from the adjoining lands—surmounted by a fence-wall of more modern date, and shaded by lofty trees. There is an entrance on one side, and near the centre stands a rough porphyritic stone about 10 feet in height, and 16

in circumference.   The dates and purposes of·
these two interesting pieces of antiquity are left
entirely to conjecture.

MAYBURGH.

"Mayburgh's mound and stones of power,
By Druids raised in magic hour."—SCOTT.

A plot of ground near the foot of Devoke Water
exhibits traces of numerous buildings in the form
of streets.   It is called the *city* of Barnscar.

Upon the summits of Grasmoor, Binsey, and
Carrock Fells, there are remains of basin-shaped
cavities, walled round, and apparently intended as
Beacons.   The Beacon, standing in the centre of
a large plantation on Penrith fell, is a more modern
erection of hewn stone, having been rebuilt in
1719, and commands extensive views of the country.   On the west side of the mountain Hardknot,
a space about two acres is encompassed by the
remains of a wall, with places of entrance on each

H 2

of the four sides.  There seem to have been towers at the different gates and corners, and several interior erections.

Stations, retaining the name of Castles, when scarcely a vestige of their works remains, are found in several places upon the mountains.  They are generally characterized by pieces of freestone, which must have been brought from a distance of several miles, at a time when the roads were very imperfectly formed.

Remains of Castles of a more permanent construction are to be seen at Kendal, Cockermouth,

RUINS OF KENDAL CASTLE.

Egremont, Brougham, Penrith, and Dacre.  Part of that at Cockermouth has been repaired, and is inhabited; the one at Dacre is used as a farm house; the rest are in various stages of decay.

Furness Abbey is situated in a narrow dell, in a fertile district of Lancashire, called Low Furness. It was founded in 1127, by Stephen, afterwards king of England, and involved in the general wreck of religious houses in 1537.  The monks were of the Cistercian order, from Normandy. The church has been upwards of 300 feet in length,

and 38 in breadth; the length of the transept near
140 feet; the height of the side walls about 54 feet.
The central tower is levelled with the side walls,
and only one of its stupendous arches left standing;
yet enough remains to shew the style of architecture, and to give some idea of its former magnificence. A few years ago, the proprietor, Lord G.
Cavendish, caused the rubbish to be cleared away:
by which many pieces of sculpture were brought
to light that had lain buried for centuries.

CALDER ABBEY.

Calder Abbey lies about four miles south of
Egremont. It was founded by the second Ra-
nulph de Meschines, about seven years after that
at Furness—on which it was dependent—and on
a much smaller scale. Some of the walls, with
the arches which supported the tower, and a part
of the colonnade, are still in good preservation.

On the banks of the river Lowther, about a
mile west of Shap, may be seen some remains of
an Abbey of still smaller dimensions; which was
founded about the year 1150.

# EXPLANATION OF PROVINCIAL TERMS.

BARROW, a term often intended to signify an artificial hill, is also applied to natural ones. There is Barrow on the west side of Derwent Lake, a hill 1200 feet high; there is Whitbarrow near Penrith, and Whitbarrow near Witherslack; Yewbarrow in Witherslack, and Yewbarrow in Wasdale. Latterbarrow explains itself—a hill branching from the side of a mountain: we have Latterbarrow at the foot of Wast Water, and Latterbarrow in Ennerdale.

KNOT, a small rocky protuberance on the side of a mountain.

COP, a little round-topped hill.

DOD is generally applied to a secondary elevation attached to one of the larger mountains; and mostly having a rounded summit. There is the Dod on the western side of Skiddaw; another in front of Red Pike; and Starling Dod, nearer Ennerdale. In the mountain range, proceeding north from Helvellyn, are Stybarrow Dod, Watson Dod, and Great Dod; and in Patterdale, Glenridding Dod, and Hartsop Dod.

How generally implies a hill rising in a valley; (the sides of such hills are frequently ornamented with dwellings.) There is the How, half way between the lakes of Derwent and Bassenthwaite; Pouter How, at the head of Bassenthwaite lake, and Castle How, at its foot; Great How near

Rosthwaite, and Great How near Leathes Water; the How and Butterlip How in Grasmere, the How in Ennerdale, and the How near Loughrigg Tarn, with several others. Numerous diluvial hillocks of a parabolic form are found in the heads of several vales—in both the Langdales, in Greenup vale in Borrowdale; and in the head of Ennerdale, where they are peculiarly interesting, especially to the geologist.

SCAR, escarpment, a range of rock; most common in limestone districts.

SCREES, a profusion of loose stones, the debris of the rocks above, resting upon a declivity as steep as is possible for them to remain; so that the least disturbance in any part communicates a motion, somewhat between sliding and rolling, which frequently extends to a distance, and takes some time before quiet is restored.

DOOR, an opening between two perpendicular cheeks of rock: as Mickle Door—Coom Door—Low Door, modernized into Lowdore.

COOM in some districts, and COVE in others, denotes a place scooped out of the side of a mountain; there is Black Coom or Comb; The Coom, and Gillercoom in Borrowdale; Keppel Cove, Brown Cove, Red Cove, Ruthwaite Cove, and others, in the side of Helvellyn.

SLACK, a lesser hollow.

FELL, the same as mountain, a large hill.

CAM [comb], the crest of a mountain, like that of a cock: as, Catsty Cam—Rosthwaite Cam.

MAN, a pile of stones on the summit of a hill.

NEESE [nose], a ridge running from the summit of a mountain steeply downwards: as, Gavel neese —Lingmell neese.

The bill of a bird is called its "neb;" so NEB, NAB, KNAB, or SNAB, like ness, naze, or neese, means a promontory or projecting piece of land, either into a lake or from the end of a mountain. There are Landing Nab and Rawlinson's Nab on Windermere, Nab Scar above Rydal Water, Nab Crag in Wythburn, and in Patterdale; Bowness on Windermere, Bowness, Broadness, and Scarness, on Bassenthwaite lake; High Snab and Low Snab in the vale of Newlands.

HAUSE, the throat, a narrow passage over a height between two mountains: as Esk-hause, Buttermere-hause.

THWAITE is a common termination to names of places, and is understood by some to signify a piece of land enclosed and cleared. We have Rosthwaite, Longthwaite, Stonethwaite, and Seathwaite, in Borrowdale; all which endings are locally pronounced long, as *Rost-whait.* Applethwaite near Windermere, and Applethwaite near Keswick, Brackenthwaite in Cumberland; Satterthwaite and Seathwaite in Lancashire; are all usually pronounced short, as *Apple-thet.*

GRANGE, a farm or habitation near the water; as Grange in Borrowdale, Grange in Bampton, Grange in Cartmel, and Marsh Grange on the river Duddon.

Holm, or Holme, an island, or a plain by the water side.

Kell or Keld, a spring of water.

Wath, a ford across a river.

Syke, in provincial dialect, is a stream of the smallest class: as Heron-Syke near Burton—dividing the counties of Westmorland and Lancashire.

Gill (sometimes wrote *Ghyll* to secure the hard sound of the *G*) is a mountain stream confined between steep banks, and running in a rapid descent. These gills are instrumental in enriching the valleys by the spoil of the mountains; they contribute to the formation of a plot of superior land on the side of a valley; or sometimes a low promontory sweeping with a bold curve into a lake.

Beck is a term used promiscuously for river, rivulet, or brook; it signifies a stream in the bottom of a vale, and to which the gills are tributary. These becks receive a name from some dale, hamlet, or some remarkable place which they pass, and in their course the appellation is frequently changed; for instance, a stream running north from Bowfell, and receiving several augmentations in its progress down Borrowdale, is called Langstreth beck; then Stonethwaite beck, Rosthwaite beck, and Grange beck, till it enters Derwent lake, thence it has the name of Derwent to Workington, where it falls into the sea.

## THE SEASON

For visiting the lakes depends much upon the taste of the Tourist. They may be seen with pleasure at any time from the beginning of May to the end of October, provided the weather be favourable. Pedestrians will feel the month of May an agreeable season, and they will then find more room at the inns. Towards the end of June, many professional gentlemen are at liberty, and students at the Universities often find it advantageous to spend three months among the lakes; thus blending instruction with healthy recreation. Large parties commonly require more time in fitting out, and are later in arrival: so that the most busy time is generally from the last week in July to the middle of September. The artist will prefer the richly diversified colouring of autumn, which will be in the greatest perfection in the month of October.

To such as make the tour with a disposition to be pleased, every season has its peculiar charms. The budding spring, the blooming summer, the luxuriant autumn, and even the biting frosts of winter, have each their respective attractions. In spring, all nature is in her most cheerful mood: it is pleasing to observe the daily progress of the various kinds of trees as they spread out their leaves, and the different plants as they expand their blossoms; while the feathered choir enliven the air with their morning and evening songs.

In the middle of summer, all is gay; the heat of the sun may at times incommode, but the lengthened days will afford a few hours for retirement in the shade, and the evenings are free from the chilling blasts prevalent at other seasons. In autumn, the fields, the woods, and the mountain sides, display the most splendid variety of colouring, and the air is often favourable for distant prospects; but the days are somewhat contracted, and for long excursions more early rising is required. Even in winter, the lakes still exhibit the same expanse of water, or else a glassy sheet of ice; the mountains—whether naked, or partially or wholly covered with a mantle of snow—still reign in their wonted majesty; the rocks have lost nothing of their grandeur, and the waterfalls are occasionally rendered more striking by the splendent and fantastic forms in which their spray is congealed.

But it should be kept in mind that more rain falls in mountainous than in open countries, and the showers come on more suddenly. The time of the tourist should, therefore, be so calculated as to allow him now and then a spare day; as there is a probability that the greatest part of a day will be sometimes of necessity spent within doors—when the museums and exhibitions of natural and artificial curiosities will be the principal resources.

# GENERAL DIRECTIONS:

## WITH NOTICES OF THE MOST INTERESTING OBJECTS PASSED IN EACH ROUTE.

---

## STAGES.

|  | MILES. |
|---|---|
| Lancaster over Sands, to Ulverston | 22 |
| Lancaster to Milnthorp | 14 |
| Milnthorp to Newby Bridge | 15 |
| Newby Bridge to Ulverston | 9 |
| Ulverston to Hawkshead | 16 |
| Hawkshead to Bowness, by the Ferry | 6 |
| Ulverston to Coniston Waterhead | 14 |
| Coniston Waterhead to Bowness, by the Ferry | 9 |
| Coniston Waterhead to Ambleside | 8 |
| Milnthorp to Kendal | 8 |
| Milnthorp to Bowness by Crosthwaite | 14 |
| Lancaster to Burton | 11 |
| Burton to Kendal | 11 |
| Kendal to Bowness | 9 |
| Bowness to Ambleside | 6 |
| Kendal to Low Wood Inn | 12 |
| Kendal to Ambleside | 14 |
| Bowness to Newby Bridge | 8 |
| Newby Bridge to Hawkshead | 9 |
| Hawkshead to Ambleside | 5 |
| Low Wood Inn to Penrith | 27 |
| Low Wood Inn to Keswick | 19 |
| Ambleside to Patterdale | 10 |
| Ambleside to Penrith | 25 |
| Ambleside to Keswick | 17 |
| Keswick to Cockermouth | 13 |
| Cockermouth to Whitehaven, by Workington | 16 |
| Keswick to Penrith | 18 |
| Penrith to Carlisle | 18 |
| Keswick to Wigton | 22 |
| Wigton to Carlisle | 11 |

In making the tour of the Lakes, various routes present themselves, the choice of which must depend upon circumstances of taste, convenience, and mode of travelling. Keswick and Ambleside are central points, from which the English Lakes and their surrounding valleys and mountains are generally visited. Keswick may be made head quarters for the Cumberland Lakes; Ambleside, for those of Westmorland and Lancashire. There are other places—as Bowness, Low Wood, Coniston Waterhead, Patterdale, and Pooley Bridge —where a few days might be employed very agreeably; and a deviation to Shap Wells might be advantageous to health, as well as recreation; and in consequence of increased facilities for travelling, the Spaw at Gilsland might also be reached at a moderate sacrifice of time or expense.

Tourists from the north may proceed from Carlisle either by Wigton or Penrith. Carlisle to Wigton is 11 miles, Wigton to Keswick 22 miles. After leaving Wigton, there are some good views over the Solway Frith to the Scottish coast and mountains; and further on, Bassenthwaite Lake, which some say should be first visited, is seen from the road— one of the richest views of the valley in which it is placed being from the top of a bank about four miles after leaving Ireby. There is also a good retrospective view about five miles before reaching Keswick. Having seen the vale of Borrowdale, the lakes of Derwent, Buttermere, Crummock, Lowes Water, Ennerdale, and Wast

Water, the mountain Skiddaw, and other objects
to be visited from Keswick, the routes to which
will be detailed hereafter, proceed by Thirlmere,
stopping at Wythburn to ascend Helvellyn, if that
be agreed on; then by Grasmere and Rydal to
Ambleside. After making excursions from thence
to Langdale, Loughrigg, and other places in the
vicinity, proceed to Coniston; thence by Hawkshead and Esthwaite Water to the Ferry on Windermere, crossing to Bowness and Ambleside; from
thence over Kirkstone to Patterdale and Ullswater, and Hawes Water, if that is to be included,
and finish the tour at Penrith, or by Bampton and
Shap to Kendal.

Tourists commencing at Penrith, may go first
to Hawes Water, either returning to Penrith or
to Pooley Bridge; then by Ullswater to Patterdale, and over Kirkstone to Ambleside, Windermere, Coniston, Langdale, Rydal, and Grasmere,
and over Dunmail Raise to Keswick; from whence,
after having made the recommended excursions,
return by Threlkeld to Penrith. Or they may
reverse the tour by driving first to Keswick, and
conclude with Ullswater or Hawes Water.

Parties landing at Whitehaven, Workington, or
Maryport, with an intention of seeing all the
lakes, and proceeding southwards, may go through
Egremont to Calder Bridge, 10 miles; from thence
by Gosforth to the Strands, 7 miles. At Strands
there are two inns, and it is about a mile and a
half further to the foot of the lake. Having seen

Wast Water, return to Calder Bridge, and by Cold Fell, or by Egremont, to Ennerdale, and by Lowes Water, Crummock, and Buttermere to Keswick; from whence, as may be found expedient, the tour may be continued to the more southern lakes.

Or this route might be reversed, by parties commencing their tour at Whitehaven, with an intention of seeing all the lakes, and concluding it at the same place; by taking first Ennerdale and Wasdale, and going from thence by Broughton to Coniston and the other lakes, reserving Buttermere, Crummock, and Lowes Water, to the last; but those who require a conveyance, will find a difficulty in procuring it on some parts of this route. Pedestrians might go from Wasdale over by Burnmoor Tarn to Eskdale, and either over Hardknot and Wrynose, or over Walney Scar to Coniston; and thence to Windermere and the other lakes, as recommended to parties from the south.

As the greatest portion of visitors come from the south, it has formerly been considered that these might safely proceed as far north as Lancaster before it became requisite to determine upon the arrangement of their progress through the district; but now that steamers have been established across Morecambe Bay, both from Liverpool and Fleetwood-on-the-Wyre, to the opposite coast of Low Furness, a decision is sooner required.

I 2

From Preston, a railway branches off to Fleet-
wood, where an elegant hotel has been erected;
from whence, at a certain time of the tide, passen-
gers are conducted by steam-boat in about an hour
and a half to Bardsea, which is three miles from
Ulverston, where conveyances can be had either
to Furness Abbey or forward to the lakes.

Pedestrians, when at Bardsea, may find some
pleasant walks, as to Conishead Priory, to Birkrigg, and thence to Furness Abbey, and by Dalton
to Ulverston.

From Preston, there is also a quick-sailing
packet-boat, which is a very steady and noiseless
conveyance, to Kendal; but the railway having
been brought as far as Lancaster, a majority of
travellers having taken their places thereon, will
continue upon it to that town.

## LANCASTER

Is a well-built town, containing 12,000 inhabitants.
It is a sea-port upon the Lune, over which there
is a handsome bridge; and about a mile further
up, a grand aqueduct, by which the Canal is conducted across the river.

The Castle, including the County jail and spacious halls for the administration of justice, occupies a commanding situation. A great part of
the building is modern; but the keep, erected by
Roger of Poitou, still remains; from the turret of
which, called John of Gaunt's Chair, is a most

extensive and beautiful prospect. An ancient Church, with a lofty tower, stands upon the same eminence. The King's Arms, Royal Oak, and Commercial, are the principal inns.

Proceeding from Lancaster, several roads lie before us. The most direct route from Lancaster is either by Burton or by Milnthorp, to Kendal, each a distance of 22 miles. Opposite the village of Bolton, about two miles to the right, is a natural cavern, called Dunald Mill Hole: it is inferior in extent and grandeur to some in the West Riding of Yorkshire and in Derbyshire; but to those who have not an opportunity of visiting others, it may give some idea of the nature of these subterranean cavities. Warton Crag on the left, and Farlton Knot on the right of the road, are two stratified hills of limestone, rising to a considerable height: the latter said to be nearly 600 feet above the road. On the Milnthorp road, the waterfall at Beetham Mill attracts the notice of the traveller.

Another line from Lancaster is up the Vale of Lune, and by Kirkby Lonsdale to Kendal. The distance is greater by 8 miles than that just mentioned; but the drive up Lunesdale is much admired. This route is more fully described in a latter portion of this work, which has special reference to Lonsdale and the Caves of Yorkshire.

Should the ruins of Furness Abbey be an object of contemplation, the shortest way is to cross the Lancaster and Ulverston Sands, which has formerly been described as a very interesting ride.

### LANCASTER TO ULVERSTON, OVER THE SANDS.

| MILES. | | MILES. |
|---|---|---|
| 4 | Hest Bank | 4 |
| 10 | Kent's Bank | 14 |
| 2 | Flookborough | 16 |
| 1 | Cark | 17 |
| 3 | Canal-foot | 20 |
| 2 | Ulverston | 22 |

Flookborough is a village lying between the estuaries of the Kent and Leven; it has two comfortable inns fitted for the reception of persons making use of a medicinal spring near Humphrey Head, two miles distant. This water is considered a mild and safe purgative; and, were suitable accommodations erected upon the spot, there would be no doubt of its becoming a place of considerable resort. On the other hand is the small town of Cartmel, with its ancient Church; between Flookborough and the Leven sands, surrounded by a fine park, lies Holker Hall, the seat of The Earl of Burlington: and on the opposite shore of the Leven are the noble woods of Conishead and Bardsea.

To avoid the sands, the crossing of which has in some instances been attended with danger, the more circuitous turnpike road by Milnthorp is now generally preferred.

From Lancaster to Milnthorp is 14 miles: and here is the option of the Ulverston or Kendal roads. After passing Heversham and Levens, the Ulverston road turns to the left, over some large tracts of peat-moss, having on the right the

isolated ridges of limestone, called Whitbarrow and
Yewbarrow, forming lofty scars on their western
sides, and reposing on the slaty rock upon which
the road in part is formed. From Milnthorp to
Newby Bridge is 15 miles; here is the choice of
continuing the Ulverston road, or proceeding along
the banks of Windermere, by Bowness and Low
Wood to Ambleside.

The road to Ulverston now follows the course
of the Leven to Backbarrow, where it crosses the
river by a bridge situated among manufactories of
cotton, of iron, of pyroligneous acid, and of gunpowder. Leaving Hollow Oak on the left, it
passes over some peat-moss, and presently approaches the sands; where it is interesting to
meet the flowing tide, as it washes against the
breastwork of the road. The river Crake, which
issues from Coniston Water, is then crossed by a
bridge under which the tide flows, and we join the
old road near a place called Green Odd; where
small craft take in their lading, consisting chiefly
of slate, timber, and iron. From Newby Bridge
to Ulverston is 9 miles.


## ULVERSTON

Is a neat market town, containing 5352 inhabitants,
and two good inns, the Sun, and the Bradyll's
Arms. It communicates with the channel of the
Leven by a canal admitting vessels of considerable
burden.

From Ulverston to Dalton is 5 miles, and from Dalton to Furness Abbey (described in a former page,) nearly 2 miles.

A mile west of the Abbey, from the top of Hawcoat, there is a prospect, over a richly culti-vated country and a part of the sea, to a most extensive range of distant mountains: and from the more lofty station of Birkrigg, the view of Furness and the surrounding coast is singularly beautiful. Two miles from Ulverston is Conis-head, generally called the Priory, a place highly extolled by Mr. West, who says, "It is a great omission in the curious traveller, to be in Furness and not to see so wonderfully pretty a place." The mansion has been several years in rebuilding, and when finished, will be a splendid residence. Ulverston is upon the slaty rock, Dalton upon mountain limestone; and the valley in which Fur-ness Abbey is placed, is flanked by red sandstone, from which the Abbey has been built. Iron ore is procured in large quantities from veins in the limestone; good specimens of red hematite are sometimes obtained, with specular iron ore, and quartz crystals.

On leaving Ulverston for the lakes, the road generally preferred leads by Lowick Chapel, where there is a good view of Coniston Lake, with the mountains at its head, and Helvellyn in the dis-tance; and after crossing Lowick Bridge, it pro-ceeds up the eastern side of the lake to Waterhead Inn, distant from Ulverston 14 miles.

At Coniston, besides the views of the lake from its banks, and from its bosom in a boat, the lovers of landscape beauties may find some pretty walks in the vales of Yewdale and Tilberthwaite. A full length view of the lake is obtained in passing over the hill called Tarnhows, on the road towards Elterwater; and an excursion to Levers Water and the Old Man, on a fine day, would not be thought uninteresting. The geologist may occupy himself in tracing a stratum of transition limestone, alternating with slate, as it bassets out upon the hills, on the north-west of the road leading towards Borwick Ground; just beyond which place this limestone has been quarried and burnt, on the left of the road to Ambleside. The slate quarries about Tilberthwaite, and the copper mines on Tilberthwaite Fell, and near Levers Water, may also be visited; and on the road to Ambleside, the Brathay flag quarry may be considered worthy of notice.

From Coniston, those who feel no hesitation in crossing the Ferry on Windermere, may proceed through Hawkshead, by the side of Esthwaite Water, to the Ferry; and after taking a view of Windermere, from Mr. Curwen's Station-house, cross the water to Bowness, distant from Coniston Water-head 9 miles. Those who object to crossing the water, may either proceed from Coniston to Ambleside direct, 8 miles; or from the Ferry, by the western banks of the lake to Ambleside, distant from Coniston by this route 14 miles.

Omitting Furness Abbey, some will proceed directly to Kendal, and from thence to Bowness, Low Wood, or Ambleside; or for such as wish to enter at once upon the centre of Windermere, there is a shorter and less hilly road from Milnthorp to Bowness, through Crosthwaite and Winster, in one stage of 14 miles. From Milnthorp to Kendal is 8 miles; the road crosses the Kent near the ancient mansion of the Howards at Levens; and passes the castellated Hall of Sizergh, the family seat of the Stricklands.

## KENDAL

Is a clean and well-built town, of considerable trade, with a population of 12,000 inhabitants. It is situate at the junction of the Carlisle road by Penrith, with the Whitehaven road by Ambleside, Keswick, and Cockermouth. It is famous for the manufacture of various kinds of woollen goods and fancy waistcoats. Here is a manufactory of ivory combs; and a marble manufactory, where several varieties of the limestone of the country, as well as foreign marbles, are worked and polished. The remains of an ancient Castle stand upon a verdant

hill on the east side of the town, which commands an extensive view over the river, the town, and adjacent country; bounded by noble ranges of mountains. On a mount on the other side of the town is an obelisk, in memory of the revolution in 1688. The King's Arms and Commercial are the principal Inns.

Hawes Water may be visited from Penrith or Kendal; and there are various mountain passes by which it may be approached by pedestrians.

A way on horseback through Long Sleddale, has been described with a high degree of colouring in some former publications; but in planning an excursion, several things are to be taken into consideration; as, what kind of conveyance the road will admit of, how that conveyance is to be supplied, and at what places refreshment may be obtained. Long Sleddale is a valley possessing all the requisites of meadows, woods, mountains, rocks, and waterfalls; but they are deficient in that harmony of composition which renders some of the more northern valleys so attractive to the tourist.

The road over Gatescarth, between Branstree and Harter Fell, is steep on both sides, yet such as a horse may be ridden, or possibly a cart may pass; and from the highest part there is an extensive view towards the sea. The way from Kentmere, over Nan Bield, between Harter Fell and High Street, is still more difficult.

Mardale Green, to which the road descends, is

K

about 15 miles from Kendal, and the same from
Penrith; it is bounded by the mountains Branstree, Harter Fell, and High Street. From the
last of which a narrow ridge called Long Stile,
projects so far as to seclude it from the other part
of the valley; and beyond this rises the apex of
Kidsey Pike. Here are two or three dwellings,
one of which is a public-house; and the Dun Bull
on Mardale Green will be no alarming or unwel-
come object to the weary traveller.

### KENDAL TO HAWES WATER, BY SHAP.

| MILES. | | MILES. |
|---|---|---|
| 8½ | High Borrow Bridge (Huck's) | 8½ |
| 7¼ | Shap | 16 |
| 4 | Bampton | 20 |
| 2 | Foot of Hawes Water | 22 |

Four miles before reaching Shap, a road turns
off to Shap Wells, at the distance of a mile. This
is stated by Mr. Alderson to be a most genial and
sanative saline spring; milder than the Harrogate
Purgative Spaw, more active than the Gilsland
Water, and in its properties nearly allied to that
of Leamington. A spacious Hotel has been erected
contiguous, with Baths, and every accommodation
for visitors. The inn lying at some distance from
the turnpike, visitors have been inconvenienced
by the want of a place for the reception of their
luggage; but this has just been remedied by the
erection of a convenient lodge by the way side,
where the services of porters may be had, and
vehicles for the conveyance of invalids.

## KENDAL TO BOWNESS AND AMBLESIDE.

To Bowness is 9 miles, to Low Wood Inn 12, and to Ambleside 14 miles.

Both these roads lead over elevated ground, from whence, looking towards the west and north-west, a most splendid arrangement of mountains is presented to the view, as delineated at page 6. On the north and east may be seen the Rydal, Troutbeck, Kentmere, and Howgill Fells, and south-east the distant table land of Ingleborough.

## BOWNESS

Stands upon a fine bay of Windermere, where boats of various descriptions may be seen riding at anchor. The walls of the houses and gardens are beautifully decorated with evergreens and flowers. The White Lion is a spacious Inn, with a neat flower garden and elevated grass plot adjoining; and the Crown is pleasantly situated upon an eminence overlooking the village. On a site equally elevated stands an elegant School-House, erected in 1836, by the late Colonel Bolton. The church possesses some painted glass, brought from Furness Abbey; and its cemetery contains the remains of the late Bishop Watson.

Near Bowness are eminences of various degrees of elevation; where views may be taken either from a higher or a lower station; and from the road between Bowness and Low Wood, is a good prospect of the lake and the mountains beyond it.

## BOWNESS TO ESTHWAITE WATER AND CONISTON.

Coniston lake and its environs may be visited from Bowness, first crossing the Ferry on Windermere, and passing beneath the *Station*, which is built upon a rock, tastefully ornamented with evergreens and flowering shrubs, and may be visited by the way. Ascending a long steep hill, there is a retrospect across the lake, backed by the wooded heights of Cartmel Fells. At the top of the hill there is a prospect of the Coniston mountains, and a mile further on, Bowfell and Langdale Pikes appear in magnificent array. There are some neat houses in the hamlet of Sawrey, and Mr. Beck has a beautiful seat at Esthwaite Lodge, on the other side of the water. Here are sweet views over the expanded valley in which the town of Hawkshead is placed, with its church upon an elevated site. The road passes on the margin of Esthwaite Water, where the Coniston, Langdale, and Grasmere mountains may be seen; and, when unobstructed by trees, the easternmost point of Skiddaw can be seen through the gap of Dunmail Raise, with Seat Sandal, Helvellyn, and Fairfield to the right hand.

Passing through the little market town of

Hawkshead, where a post-chaise is kept at the Red Lion, the road lies over high grounds, and has a steep descent to the inn at Coniston Waterhead, distant from Bowness 9 miles. Round the head of the lake there is a beautiful admixture of wood and grass lands, swelling in fine undulations. By taking a boat half way down the lake, its principal beauties are unfolded; and the return may be made either by the head of Windermere to Bowness, 13, or to Ambleside, 8 miles: but it would be a great omission to forego the beautiful views that might be had on the road from Bowness, by Troutbeck bridge and Low Wood, to Ambleside.

## LOW WOOD INN

Is a convenient place to take a boat upon the lake of Windermere, and the high ground above it commands excellent views. A pleasing excursion, on foot, may be made by taking the turnpike road towards Ambleside, about a mile and a half, to Low Fold, where a road turns off, ascending to High Skelgill, thence by Low Skelgill, to the Troutbeck road, by which return to Low Wood; in the whole about five miles. From High Skelgill the walk might be extended to Wansfell Pike. From a place near the junction of the Skelgill and Troutbeck roads, may be observed one of the most enchanting scenes among the lakes; comprehending the most perfect view of all the islands on Windermere, separated by the most desirable

к 2

spaces; the lake spread out into beautiful bays, and its shores ornamented with elegant villas, planted on various elevations. Excursions may also be made from Low Wood, to Coniston, to Langdale, or over Kirkstone to Ullswater.

Here, while the admirer of landscape takes his views of the lake and mountain scenery from the rising ground, and the angler amuses himself upon the water, the geologist may be employed in examining the position of the transition limestone and the slate, where they have been worked, in two adjoining quarries near the road, about a quarter of a mile north of the inn.

## AMBLESIDE

Is an ancient chartered town, with a population of 1100; but its market is little more than nominal. It is irregularly built, upon a rising ground, commanding good prospects of the adjacent scenery.

MILLS AT AMBLESIDE.

Post-chaises are kept at the Salutation and Commercial Inns, and there are other public-houses that accomodate travellers; besides several houses fitted up as private lodgings. Boats upon the lake of Windermere are also provided by the inns.

### FROM AMBLESIDE TO LANGDALE.

| MILES. | | MILES. |
|---|---|---|
| 3 | Skelwith Bridge | 3 |
| 2 | Colwith Cascade | 5 |
| 3 | Blea Tarn | 8 |
| 3 | Dungeon Gill | 11 |
| 2 | Langdale Chapel Stile | 13 |
| 5 | By High Close and Rydal to Ambleside. | 18 |

The Langdale excursion from Ambleside or Low Wood, presents a variety of lake and mountain scenery, scarcely to be equalled in a journey of the same length, during the whole tour. It was formerly performed chiefly on horseback, but carriages adapted to the road can now be obtained, and are more frequently employed. Passing Clappersgate, the party may either proceed with the river on the left, to Skelwith Bridge; or crossing Brathay Bridge, take the river on the right, by Skelwith Fold; the latter may be recommended to pedestrians. At Skelwith Bridge is a public-house, and, a little further up the river, a capacious waterfall; but the road by Skelwith Fold, being on a higher elevation, commands a fuller view into Great Langdale. After the junction of the two roads, there is a view of Elterwater. The road entering Lancashire at Brathay, or at Skelwith

Bridge, leaves it again at Colwith Bridge; a little above which is a splendid cascade. After passing Little Langdale Tarn, the ancient pack-horse road, from Kendal to Whitehaven over Wrynose, takes the left hand; the one to be pursued turns to the right, ascending the common to Blea Tarn; near to which the Langdale Pikes exhibit their most magnificent contour. Leaving the tarn and solitary farm-house—the scene of Wordsworth's "Recluse"—on the left, proceed to the edge of the hill, where you will have a fine view of the head of Great Langdale, into which the road steeply descends. A stream issuing between the two Pikes, and falling among broken felspathic rocks, constitutes the noted waterfall called Dungeon Gill. Mill Beck the stream flowing from Stickle Tarn, gives name to two farm houses, at one of which it may be convenient to leave the horses, while visiting Dungeon Gill. Following the road down Great Langdale, the traveller will arrive at Thrang Crag, where the rock in a slate quarry is excavated in an awful manner; and soon after pass the chapel, near which is a small ale-house. Here parties on horseback, taking the road to the left, come to a second prospect of Elterwater; and near the farm-house called High Close, there is a fine view over Loughrigg Tarn, with Windermere in the distance; then crossing a road leading from Skelwith Bridge, we come in sight of the peaceful vale of Grasmere, near the station recommended by Mr. West. The road from thence is formed along the skirts of

Loughrigg Fell, in a kind of terrace, from whence there is a rich view of the lake and vale of Grasmere on the left. Further on, the road approaches Rydal Water, and soon after passing that, and the village of Rydal, the turnpike road is joined, and, in a mile more, the excursion is concluded at Ambleside, after a most pleasing circuit of eighteen miles. Parties in carriages are obliged to hold to the right from the chapel to the gunpowder works; then to the left towards Loughrigg Tarn; and from thence by Clappersgate to Ambleside.

A variety of shorter excursions may be made from Ambleside; a walk of seven hundred yards from the inn, to the waterfall of Stock Gill, should not be neglected; and one of a mile and a half may be taken to the falls of Rydal. A ramble round the lakes of Rydal and Grasmere—round or over Loughrigg Fell—a more elevated walk to Wansfell Pike—or the still more lofty circuit of Fairfield, on a favourable opportunity—will not fail to please such as delight in extensive prospects. Those who have not already seen Coniston, may take an excursion thither; and Ullswater may also be visited from hence, by the steep carriage road over Kirkstone. Some who travel on horseback may choose a ride over the mountains Wrynose and Hardknot, through the vale of Eskdale to the Strands in Nether Wasdale, about 24 miles; and next day by Wast Water, Styhead, and Borrowdale, to Keswick, 20 miles.

## AMBLESIDE TO LOUGHRIGG FELL, AND LOUGHRIGG TARN.

It is a pleasant stroll for a pedestrian through the fields to Miller Bridge, from whence a path leads over the lower part of the fell. After reaching the open common, a tourist of taste will not be confined to the path, but, by rambling from knoll to knoll, will obtain a most pleasing variety of prospects; and on reaching the top of Ivy Crag, a large rock overlooking Loughrigg Tarn, he will have an instantaneous burst upon a most extraordinary assemblage of landscape beauties. Returning from the top of the rock, and proceeding by the path, he will soon perceive Loughrigg Tarn in the best position for a picture; having Langdale Pikes in the distance. Leaving Loughrigg Tarn on the right hand, he may follow the road towards Grasmere, past the house called Scroggs, till he gain a sight of Grasmere lake; then turning off to the right, he will enjoy the beautiful views of Grasmere and Rydal, from the terrace road mentioned in a former page; and for such as have not included this part of the road in a former excursion, it may be highly recommended; a walk altogether of about seven or eight miles. Or, on leaving Ivy Crag, he may traverse over the highest part of the fell; and make the descent towards Rydal.

Those who travel in carriages may go by Clappersgate, leaving Loughrigg Tarn and Grasmere Lake both on the right hand, and Grasmere Church on the left; returning on the eastern side of the

two lakes, by the hamlet of Rydal to Ambleside—
an excursion of ten miles. If required, a deviation
may be made to Skelwith Force, or into Great
Langdale, as far as Millbeck and Dungeon Gill.

### AMBLESIDE TO ULLSWATER.

| MILES. | | MILES. |
|---|---|---|
| 4 Top of Kirkstone ... . .. .......... ..... | | 4 |
| 3 Kirkstone foot ............... . ......... | | 7 |
| 3 Inn at Patterdale ...... ........... ...... | | 10 |

This is a very steep carriage road, rising 1300
feet from Ambleside, and falling 900 feet on the
other side. This hill has taken its name of Kirkstone from a detached mass of rock, standing at a
little distance from the road, and bearing some
resemblance to the form of a house. The road
passes close to the edge of Brothers Water, which
in character approaches that of a lake; although
its dimensions are not greater than some of the
mountain tarns: the level meadows on the further
side are bordered by native woods, surmounted by
precipitous rocks: the road then leads through a
narrow but pleasant valley to the inn at Patterdale.
Here a boat may be taken upon Ullswater, after
which the return may be made the same way; or
from Patterdale the carriage may be driven along
the side of Ullswater to Penrith, 15 miles. Or it
may sometimes be preferred to stop at Pooley
Bridge, from whence Lowther Castle and Hawes
Water may be visited. Or turning to the left in
Gowbarrow Park, by Matterdale, Hutton Moor,
and Threlkeld, to Keswick, 20 miles.

## AMBLESIDE TO ESKDALE AND WASDALE.

| MILES. | | MILES. |
|---|---|---|
| 3 | Skelwith Bridge | 3 |
| 1½ | Colwith | 4½ |
| 2½ | Fellfoot | 7 |
| 2 | Top of Wrynose | 9 |
| 2 | Cockley Beck . | 11 |
| 4 | Dawson Ground, Wool Pack | 15 |
| 3½ | King of Prussia | 18½ |
| 3 | Santon Bridge . . | 21½ |
| 2½ | Strands, Nether Wasdale | 24 |

This tour may be made on horseback, or, with some little difficulty, in a cart; taking the road to Little Langdale, as before described, and following the old pack-horse road over Wrynose and Hardknot, both of which hills are very steep. Near the road on Wrynose are the three shire stones of Cumberland, Westmorland, and Lancashire. From Westmorland we here pass into Lancashire; and crossing the head of the Duddon at Cockley-beck, we enter into Cumberland. From the top of Hardknot there is a view of the sea, and the Isle of Man, in the horizon; and half way down the hill on the right, are the ruins of a place called Hardknot Castle; but having been built without mortar or cement, scarcely any part of the walls are left standing.

The small river Esk winds along a narrow valley, among verdant fields, surmounted by rugged rocks, and about a mile and a half down the valley is a public-house, formerly the sign of the Wool Pack, about 15 miles from Ambleside. On the left hand, in travelling down the valley, there are two remarkable cascades. The first is seen from

the road; but the other, which lies beyond the
chapel, requires a walk of more than half a mile
to view it. From the hamlet of Bout, a dim track
leads over Burnmoor to Wasdale Head; but the
road should be kept nearly to Santon Bridge,
when it turns off to the right, to the Strands at
Nether Wasdale; where there are two public-
houses. After seeing Wast Water, parties on
horseback may go over Styhead, and through
Borrowdale, to Keswick; with a cart, it will be
necessary to go by Gosforth to Calder Bridge;
from thence by Ennerdale Bridge and Lamplugh
to Scale Hill, and thence either by Buttermere or
Lorton to Keswick. Sometimes this excursion
has been varied, by returning from Wasdale, by
Ulpha, to Broughton, and thence by Coniston to
Ambleside.

BRIDGE HOUSE, AMBLESIDE.

L

## AMBLESIDE TO KESWICK.

The route from Ambleside to Keswick lies through the midst of lake and mountain scenery. At one mile from Ambleside, a road crossing Pelter Bridge, on the left, leads to Langdale, or round Loughrigg Fell. To the right, among ancient oaks, stands Rydal Hall, the patrimonial residence of Lady le Fleming, who has built and endowed a neat chapel in the village. Above the chapel is Rydal Mount, the residence of the poet Wordsworth; and beyond the hall, the Rydal Waterfalls. The next object is Rydal Water, with the heronry upon one of its islands; and a little further, the extensive slate quarry of Whitemoss. The road is then conducted to the margin of Grasmere Water, and gives a good view of that admired vale. At the further end of which, between the branches of Easdale and Greenburn, stands Helm Crag, distinguished, not so much by its height, as by its summit of broken rocks, which Mr. Gray likens to "some gigantic building demolished;" Mr. West, to "a mass of antediluvian ruins;" Mr. Green, to the figures of a "lion and a lamb;" Mr. Wordsworth, to an "astrologer and an old woman cowering;" Mr. Budworth, to "a number of stones jumbled together after the mys-

tical manner of the Druids;" Mrs. Radcliffe says,
"Helm Crag rears its crest—a strange fantastic
summit, round, yet jagged and splintered;" and
the traveller who views it from Dunmail Raise,
may think that a mortar elevated for throwing shells
into the valley, would be no unapt comparison. A
road turns off on the left to the church and the Red
Lion Inn; the Swan is on the turnpike road, at the
distance of four miles and a half from Ambleside.

The long hill of Dunmail Raise is next to be
ascended. It rises to the height of 750 feet above
the level of the sea; and yet it is the lowest pass
through a chain of mountains which extends from
Black Comb, on the southern verge of Cumberland, into the county of Durham. Having over-
come the steepest part of the road, Skiddaw begins
to shew his venerable head in the distance; and
here is a retrospect over Grasmere vale, and
through a vista of mountains, extending as far as
Hampsfield Fell, near the sands of Lancaster.
At the highest part of the road, a wall separates
the counties of Westmorland and Cumberland;
and a large heap of stones is said to be the cairn,
or sepulchre, of Dunmail, last king of Cumberland, who was defeated here by the Saxon monarch, Edmund, about the year 945. The lake
Thirlmere, or Leathes' Water, now comes in view,
and the road passes between the inn and the chapel of Wythburn; about eight miles and a half
from Ambleside, and the same distance from Keswick. The mountain Helvellyn is now upon the

right; but the road lies so near its base, that the full height of the mountain cannot be seen. After passing a little way upon the margin of the lake, we come to another steep ascent, where Armboth-house, the residence of Mr. Jackson, on the other side of the water, is a good object. Dalehead Hall, the manorial seat of Mr. Leathes, stands on this side of the water, but is hid from us by an intervening hill. Having passed the summit, there is a delightful view through the vale of Legberthwaite, with its prolongation of Fornside, and Wanthwaite—together constituting what is commonly called St. John's Vale—beyond which the lofty Saddleback, with its furrowed front, closes the scene.

There is a public-house at the King's Head, six miles from Keswick, and a road turns off on the right towards Threlkeld, passing under the massive rock of Green Crag, sometimes called the Castle Rock of St. John's. Near this, a tremendous thunderstorm, in 1749, swept away a mill, and buried one of the millstones amongst the ruins, so that it has never yet been discovered.

The Keswick road inclines to the left, and, surmounting the cultivated ridge called Castlerigg, there is a full view of Derwent Lake, with part of that of Bassenthwaite, the town and vale of Keswick, with its surrounding mountains. It was here that Mr. Gray, on leaving Keswick, found the scene so enchanting, that he "had almost a mind to have gone back again."

## PENRITH

Is a good market town, with 6561 inhabitants. It is a considerable thoroughfare, being situated at the junction of the Yorkshire and Lancashire roads to Carlisle and Glasgow. The principal inns are the Crown and the George. From Penrith to Alston Moor is 20 miles, to Appleby 14, to Carlisle 18, to Kendal by Shap 27, to Keswick 18.

Ullswater may be visited from Penrith, going either by Eamont Bridge and Tirrel, or by Dalemain, to the inn at Pooley Bridge, 6 miles; with carriages, the former road is generally preferred.

Pooley Bridge is a desirable station for the lovers of angling, or to take a boat for viewing the scenery of Ullswater. During the first part of the voyage, the banks of the lake are cultivated, and adorned with several handsome villas; the mountains, right and left, are humble; but in front there is a full view of the "mighty Helvellyn." On the second reach of the lake, the mountains on the left make a nearer approach, and the shore on the right becomes more wooded. The boat may proceed to the head of the lake at Patterdale, or by the way be landed at Lyulph's Tower, for the view of Airey Force; from whence the third division, or head of the lake, is surrounded by the lofty and romantic mountains of Patterdale. Or the carriage may be driven by Watermillock, and by the side of the lake through Gowbarrow Parks,

L 2

by Lyulph's Tower, to the inn at Patterdale, distant from Penrith 15 miles.

From Patterdale, either return the same way to Penrith, or pass by Brothers Water, and over the very steep hill of Kirkstone, to Ambleside, 10 miles; or otherwise turn off in Gowbarrow Park, by Dockray and Hutton Moor, to Keswick, 20 miles.

It will generally be found most convenient to visit Hawes Water from Penrith, by way of Eamont Bridge; turning to the right at Arthur's Round Table, to Askham, 5 miles; thence by Helton, and Butterswick, to Bampton, nearly 5 more. From many parts of the road, the Castle and noble woods of Lowther, with the lofty limestone rocks of Knipe Scar, are important objects.

Leaving Bampton Grange, with its church, on the left hand, two miles more bring us in sight of Hawes Water. Some will content themselves with travelling a couple of miles along the banks of the lake, and thence return to the Grange for refreshment. At this place there are two public-houses; one of which has been rebuilt, and fitted up in a commodious manner.

Those who wish to penetrate the hidden recesses of the mountains, may go the whole length of the lake, and afterwards pass the chapel of Mardale, which is a small building closely embowered with yews and sycamores, its walls exhibiting some neat monumental inscriptions; particularly one to the memory of one of its ministers, who died in 1799, having served the cure upwards of fifty years. Here the mountains seem to forbid all further progress; but turning the end of the hill, the party will soon arrive at Mardale Green; from whence they may either return the same way, or pass over the mountains to Long Sleddale or to Kentmere.

Having viewed the lake and its accompanying scenery, the party may either return to Penrith or into the Great North Road at Shap. But to such as make this excursion on foot, or on horseback, it will be found a pleasing variety to turn off the road to the left a little before arriving at Helton, and follow a track over the common called Moor Dovack, which affords a fine view of Ullswater and its neighbouring scenery; and at Pooley Bridge is a commodious inn, from whence the road may be taken by Dalemain to Penrith. Parties taking up their quarters for a few days at Pooley Bridge, may visit Hawes Water, and Lowther Castle, the magnificent seat of the Earl of Lonsdale, most conveniently from thence.

LOWTHER CASTLE.

## COCKERMOUTH

Is a good market town with 4935 inhabitants. It possesses an ancient castle, has a handsome bridge over the river Cocker, which runs through the town to join the Derwent; and the Globe is an inn furnished with every requisite accommodation for travellers.

Parties from Cockermouth visiting the three lakes of Lowes Water, Crummock, and Buttermere, will find it the most eligible way by Pardshaw, Mockerin, and Fangs; by which the lake of Lowes Water is seen in combination with lofty mountains; and the road from thence to Scale Hill affords excellent views of Crummock Lake, with the surrounding mountains. From Cockermouth to Scale Hill by this route is about 11 miles.

After visiting Crummock and Buttermere, the party may either proceed through Newlands to Keswick, or return through the pleasant vale of Lorton to Cockermouth; and next morning, by the side of Bassenthwaite Lake to Keswick.

## KESWICK.

Having by different roads conducted the several parties to Keswick, it must be made head quarters for a while, to examine the curiosities of the place —to enjoy the rich scenery in its neighbourhood— and to make excursions, some of a few hours, some of a day, and others perhaps of more than one day.

Keswick has near 2400 inhabitants. Woollen goods and black-lead pencils are the chief manufactures. The principal inns are the Royal Oak and Queen's Head; there are other houses where parties may be accommodated, besides many neatly furnished private lodgings. Here are two museums, exhibiting the natural history of the country, and numerous foreign curiosities: one was established by the late Mr. Crosthwaite, and is now kept by his son; the other is kept by a daughter of the late Thomas Hutton, who died in 1831, at the age of 85; specimens of minerals are kept on sale at both. Mr. Wright has a good assortment of geological, mineralogical, botanical, and marine specimens, and Messrs. Cooper a brilliant collection of minerals—all on sale. A faithful Model of the Lake District, on a scale of three inches to a mile, constructed and exhibited by Mr. Flintoft, is well deserving inspection. The Rock Harmonicon, a series of pieces of stone, collected in the neighbourhood, arranged in rows, and tuned to a musical scale by William Bowe, will astonish the ear of the auditor by the sweet tones given out by so uncouth an instrument. A circulating library is kept by Mr. Bailey. Post chaises, ponies, and jaunting-cars may be had at the inns, with experienced guides for excursions by land; and neat pleasure-boats, with intelligent boatmen, for the water.

The town of Keswick is, with the adjacent valleys, included in the parish of Crosthwaite; the

church is situated at the distance of three quarters
of a mile from the centre of the town, and is a
prominent feature in the landscape.   The vicarage
has been erected upon a chosen spot, a rising
ground about a quarter of a mile from the parish
church, commanding excellent views; and Dove-
cote, the residence of James Stanger, Esq., has a
site equally favoured.   Greta Hall, the abode of
the Poet Laureate, stands upon a delightful eminence at the north end of the town.   Saint John's
church, a neat structure of hewn stone, from a
quarry at Lamonby, occupies a commanding situation at the south-east end of the town; it was opened
for divine service on the ninth of September, 1838.
The building was commenced by the late Mr.
Marshall, and by his widow completed and endowed.   A neat parsonage-house and a school-
house have also been erected by members of the
family.   T. S. Spedding, Esq., occupies a neat
house at Greta Bank; and Mrs. Turner's, at
Derwent Hill, between the lakes of Derwent and
Bassenthwaite, has a view to both.

CASTLEHEAD, (pronounced Castlet,) a wooded
rock in the centre of the Derwentwater estate,
rising 280 feet above the lake, is an excellent
station for an introduction to the beauties of Keswick vale.   From the Borrowdale road, at one
third of a mile from the inn, a path turns off by
which the hill is ascended; and from its summit
the lake of Derwent is finely displayed, with its
numerous bays and islands.   Lord's Island, near

the shore, was once the residence of the family of
Derwentwater; the smaller island of Rampsholm
lies beyond it; St. Herbert's Isle nearer the middle
of the lake; and to the right the Vicar's Isle, on
which James Henry, Esq., has a beautiful residence. The circumjacent mountains of Borrowdale and Newlands make a fine panorama. At the
head of Borrowdale appears Great End Crag, beyond it a part of Scawfell, with the highest of the
Pikes. Looking through the vale of Newlands,
Red Pike, distinguished by its colour, rises over
Buttermere. To the eastward, Wanthwaite Crags,
and Great Dod, form the end of the mountain
range extending from Helvellyn. To the north,
Skiddaw rises finely, and Saddleback may be seen
over the trees. Crosthwaite Church is a good
object in the vale, and over the rising ground
beyond Bassenthwaite Lake, the mountain Crif-
Fell, in Scotland, shews his head. This may be
thought too elevated a station for the eye of a
painter; but as a general view of the lake, the
town, and the valley, it is excellent. Some of the
lower stations, formerly recommended, are rendered less inviting by the too great profusion of
wood upon the shores of the lake, and upon its
islands; but this rock will always remain sufficiently
prominent for a prospect: and at the same time a
study for the geologist.

A walk of half a mile to the water side, with a
continuation of a quarter of a mile along it to FRIAR
CRAG, is the favourite promenade of the inhabitants

of the town, and affords much gratification to strangers. Turning to the right from the road leading to Borrowdale, the prospect is over Crow Park, to the valley and mountains of Newlands, with High-stile presiding over Buttermere in the distance: in retrospect, Skiddaw rises majestically over the town. Crow Park, now a fine, swelling, verdant field, was once a wood of stately oaks, but cut down about the year 1750. Cockshot, lying on the left, is a hill covered with trees, which intercept the views from its summit, but a walk round its margin may sometimes be taken on account of the shelter it affords. Coming in sight of the lake, Vicar's Isle is most happily placed, the house just appearing through the variegated foliage of the trees. Along the margin of the water, numerous boats are moored, some belonging to private individuals, others kept for the accommodation of visitors; and, at the termination of the walk on the low promontory of Friar Crag, the eye is saluted with a full prospect of the lake, bounded by the celebrated mountains of Borrowdale. To the left, near the shore, Stable Hills farm is reared upon the site where stood Lord Derwentwater's stables at the time his mansion was upon the adjacent island. The Parks, part cultivated, part wooded, occupy the rising ground, over which Wallow Crag shews his massive rocky front; those, with the lands betwixt the town and lake, form the Derwentwater estate, for some time belonging to Greenwich Hospital, but purchased by the late

John Marshall, jun., Esq. Further on lies Barrow House, the property of J. Pocklington, Esq., and above it the pastoral farm of Ashness; beyond the small island of Rampsholm pours the far-famed cataract of Lowdore; and Castle Crag appears between the more lofty mountains of Brund Fell and Gait Crag, like a centinel placed to guard the entrance of Borrowdale. To the right of St. Herbert's Isle, Catbells with front of brighter green, shelve down towards the lake; which is chiefly bordered on that side by the woods of the late Lord William Gordon, now Sir John Woodford's. Looking through the lateral vale of Newlands, Red Pike appears beyond Buttermere; and more to the right, Causey Pike and Grisedale Pike shew their aspiring peaks; the pass of Whinlatter, and the mountains of Thornthwaite lying still further to the right.

Excellent views of the vale and mountains are also obtained from the Vicarage, from Ormathwaite, from many parts of a road leading by Applethwaite and Millbeck, along a pleasant elevation at the foot of Skiddaw, and from the side of Latrigg. Those who admire more extensive prospects, may climb to the top of Latrigg—Wallow Crag—Swinside—Catbells—Causey Pike—Grisedale Pike, or Grasmoor; and to crown the whole, for once, to the summit of Skiddaw, Helvellyn, or the still more lofty station of Scawfell Pike.

A voyage round Derwent lake will agreeably

M

fill up a space of two or three hours in any part of
a seasonable day, and is generally thought particularly refreshing after the fatigues of a morning's
ascent of Skiddaw.   Passing Friar's Crag, a fine
bay opens out, shewing, on the left, the wooded
rock of Castlehead, with Saddleback beyond it; in
front, the Lord's Island, with the wooded steeps
of Wallow Crag; and coasting under the lofty
Falcon Crag, the boat may be landed to view the
cascades at Barrow and Lowdore, and return by
the western side of the lake.

### ROUND DERWENT LAKE.

| MILES | | MILES. |
|---|---|---|
| 2 | Barrow House, and Cascade... . ......... | 2 |
| 1 | Lowdore,        ditto  .................... | 3 |
| 1 | Grange ...................................... | 4 |
| 1 | Bowder Stone ....  ......  .................. | 5 |
| 1 | Return, and cross the River at Grange ... | 6 |
| 4½ | Portinscale  ........  ...................  ..... | 10½ |
| 1½ | Keswick  ...............  ................. | 12 |

A delightful excursion may be made round Derwent lake, either on horseback or in a carriage.
The road lies at the foot of the wooded park of
Derwentwater, with the lake on the right, and the
lofty rocks of Wallow Crag and Falcon Crag on
the left; and in many places it commands excellent
views.   One that has been much admired, till ob-
scured by extended plantings, is on emerging
from the wood to the more open common, where
the road lies just above the margin of the lake.
Two miles from Keswick, a road on the left leads
to Watendlath, and we pass the beautiful mansion

of Barrow. A fine cascade behind the house may be seen by strangers on application at the lodge. Another mile brings us to Lowdore—famous for its waterfall. Here is a neat public-house, where a cannon is kept for the echo, which is very fine, especially in a still evening. Rather more than four miles from Keswick, we have the hamlet called the Grange, upon the opposite bank of the river.

About Lowdore and Grange, the draftsman will find employment for his pencil; and the geologist will observe the transition, from the blackish clay slate upon which he treads, to the more variously aggregated and paler-coloured rocks on his left hand and before him.

The bridge at Grange might be crossed, as the shortest route; but it may be recommended to proceed forward another mile to the Bowder Stone— a fragment of rock above twenty yards in length, and half as much in height,—remarkable for being curiously poised upon one of its angles, like a ship upon its keel, with a little more support towards one end. Its weight has been variously computed

BOWDER STONE.

from 1771 to 1971 tons.   But it is not merely for the sight of this stone, that travellers are advised to advance so far.   It is chiefly for the prospect here obtained into the interior of Borrowdale, which expands itself as far as Rosthwaite; beyond which the vale is divided into two parts, the one branching off towards Grasmere and Langdale, the other towards Wasdale and Buttermere.

Returning to Grange, the road then crosses the river, and is carried along a pleasant elevation above the lead mines and woods of Brandlehow and Water End, or Derwentwater Bay, the house standing sweetly sheltered on the margin of the lake.   From this elevation, the lake, with its islands, bays, and promontories, is seen to great advantage.   The road then crossing the pleasant vale of Newlands, joins the Cockermouth road at Portinscale, and reaches Keswick in a circuit of 12 miles.

## TO BORROWDALE BY WATENDLATH.

On a second excursion to Borrowdale, on foot or on horseback, the road by Ashness to Watendlath may be taken.   From a bridge above Barrow Cascade, there is a splendid view of the valley, with the lakes of Derwent and Bassenthwaite; and a little further on, by deviating to the edge of a precipice on the right, the waterfall of Lowdore comes in view, and the lake appears at an awful depth beneath your feet.   After losing sight of the lakes, the road lies along a contracted valley, by the side of the stream which supplies the cataract of Lowdore. At the distance of five miles from Keswick, it reaches Watendlath, which consists of a few antiquated cottages and farm buildings; just beyond which the tarn is placed, amidst a small area of green meadows, surrounded by wild and uncultivated hills. A track leads from thence over the hill, from which there is a fine view of the head of Borrowdale; it then descends steeply to Rosthwaite, whence the return may be made by Bowder Stone to Keswick; a circuit of 14 miles. To contract this excursion, the stream from Watendlath may be crossed about a mile beyond Ashness; then turning towards Lowdore, there is a magnificent view of Derwent Water and Bassenthwaite through the opening above the waterfall, which may be taken at pleasure from a higher or a lower station; so as to embrace a larger or smaller portion of the lake and its islands.

### KESWICK TO BUTTERMERE.

| MILES | | MILES. |
|---|---|---|
| 5 | Bowder Stone | 5 |
| 1 | Rosthwaite | 6 |
| 2 | Seatoller | 8 |
| 2 | Honister Crag | 10 |
| 2 | Gatesgarth | 12 |
| 2 | Buttermere | 14 |
| 9 | Through Newlands to Keswick | 23 |

An excursion through Borrowdale to Buttermere may be made on horseback, or in a car adapted to the road, taking the route before de-

scribed as far as Bowder Stone: a mile beyond
which, at Rosthwaite, is a small public-house.  A
little further, a road on the left leads by Stonethwaite, over the steep mountain pass called the
Stake, to Langdale.   Tourists have sometimes
been advised, by this track, to connect Borrowdale with Langdale, in one excursion; but the
better way is to explore Langdale from Ambleside, and Borrowdale from Keswick.

At Seatoller, about eight miles from Keswick,
a road on the left leads to the black-lead mine,
and to Wast Water; and here the Buttermere
road, turning to the right, ascends, by the side of
a stream broken into pretty waterfalls, up a steep
hill; from which there are some fine retrospective
views of the upper parts of Borrowdale; and
Helvellyn soon begins to shew his head over the
mountains of Watendlath.   In passing the hause,
(which rises 800 feet above the level of Derwent
Lake,) Honister Crag, in majestic grandeur, is
presented to the view; between which and Yew
Crag, the road now sharply descends.   Both these
rocks are famed for producing roofing slate of the
best quality; and the edges of the road are beautifully tufted with *Alchemilla alpina*.  Gatesgarth
dale, through which the road now goes, (twice
crossing and re-crossing the stream,) is a narrow
valley strewed with large blocks of stone, fallen
from the rocks above; and solemnly shaded by the
lofty Honister, which towers to the height of 1700
feet above the valley at its foot.  We now re-enter

upon the same soft clay-slate rock which we parted from at Grange, and the change is soon apparent in the smoothness of the road.

Opposite to the farm of Gatesgarth, which is two miles from the inn at Buttermere, a shepherd's path leads over the mountain, by a pass called Scarf-gap, and after crossing the narrow dale of Ennerdale, proceeds to Wasdale Head over a second and higher mountain called the Black Sail. The crags on the left of Scarf-gap are, from their form, called Haystacks; and to the right, three adjoining summits are called High-crag, High-stile, and Red-pike. The two first are composed of what some would call a porphyritic greenstone rock, the third of a reddish sienite: and between the second and third lies Burtness Tarn.

The road, after passing Gatesgarth, touches upon the margin of Buttermere Lake, and a little further upon the left is the neat sheltered cottage of Haseness; and another mile brings us to the inn at Buttermere, distant from Keswick, by this route, 14 miles.

Facing the inn, on a rocky site, formerly occupied by a miniature chapel, a new one, not much larger, has been erected in 1810, at the expense of a stranger, The Rev. Vaughan Thomas, of Oxford.

At Buttermere, a boat is usually taken upon Crummock Lake, as well for the views of the scenery as being the most convenient way of seeing Scale Force. It is an agreeable walk of half

a mile to the water, and after a pleasant little
voyage of nearly a mile, a walk of three-quarters
of a mile reaches to the fall.    Travellers may
indeed walk from the inn to Scale Force; but the
path being wet and unpleasant, a boat is greatly
to be preferred.    If the weather be unfavourable
for using the boat, a good view of Crummock
Lake may be had, by riding a mile and a half on
the eastern side, to the rocky point called the Hause.
After the necessary refreshment at Buttermere, it
is an agreeable ride of 9 miles through the peaceful
vale of Newlands, and by Portinscale to Keswick.

On leaving Buttermere, we encounter a steep
hill; but the road, as well as the mountain side, is
much smoother than the ascent from Borrowdale.
In about a mile and a half we reach the top of the
Hause, and suddenly glance upon the further edge
of Derwent Water, with the wooded rock of Castlehead, and the mountain Saddleback.    The first
part of the descent into the vale of Newlands is
steep, but the road soon becomes smooth and pleasant.    From the foot of Rawling End we gain a
beautiful view over Derwent Lake and the vale of
Keswick; and join the Cockermouth road at Portinscale.

Should any objection arise to the road through
Newlands, the excursion may be prolonged by the
side of Crummock Lake, where Melbreak is a fine
object on the opposite shore, and, passing the
precipitous Grasmoor, turn to the left to Scale
Hill, and thence to Keswick or Cockermouth.

## DRIVE TO SCALE HILL, AND BUTTERMERE.

| MILES. | | MILES. |
|---|---|---|
| 2½ | Braithwaite | 2½ |
| 2½ | Summit of Whinlatter | 5 |
| 3 | Lorton | 8 |
| 4 | Scale Hill | 12 |
| 4 | Buttermere | 16 |
| 9 | Through Newlands to Keswick | 25 |

The best way for a carriage to Scale Hill or Buttermere, is by the old road towards Cockermouth over the steep mountain Whinlatter, which in the length of two miles rises to the height of 800 feet above the valley. After passing the sixth milestone, a road turns to the left, crossing a brook and winding round the end of a hill, where a fine view is presented over the cultivated vale of Lorton, and as far as the distant mountains of Kirkcudbright.

At Scale Hill, a boat may be taken on Crummock Lake, from whence the mountains surrounding that and Buttermere, may be seen to great advantage. The party may be landed for a view of Scale Force, and again for a walk to the village of Buttermere, and a view of the lake from a hill near it—returning the same way to Keswick. But should there be any objection to taking a boat, the carriage may be driven along the side of Crummock Lake, to the inn at Buttermere, and the return made through the vale of Newlands, by the road described in the last page; which requires steady horses, as it rises the height of 760 feet in less distance than a mile and a half.

## KESWICK TO WAST WATER.

| MILES. | | MILES. |
|---|---|---|
| 3 | To Scatoller ........................... | 8 |
| 1 | Seathwaite ... ..... .. ............... | 9 |
| 3 | Sty Head ........ ...................... | 12 |
| 2 | Wasdale Head ....... .. ............... | 14 |
| 6 | Nether Wasdale, Strands ............ | 20 |
| 4 | Gosforth ....... ...................... | 24 |
| 3 | Calder Bridge ........................ | 27 |

Tourists, who have no objection to the saddle, will generally be much gratified by an excursion on horseback for two days: by which plan, Borrowdale and Wast Water are seen on the first day; and Ennerdale, Lowes Water, Crummock, and Buttermere on the second. The road up Borrowdale, as far as Scatoller, has already been described; from whence the Wasdale road is on the left to Seathwaite; opposite to which, on the right, lies the famous Black-lead Mine. Carriages may be used as far as Seathwaite, but beyond that, the road becomes a mere track, fit only for horses accustomed to the country. A waterfall presents itself to view on the right; and after crossing a rude bridge, the ascent of the mountain is commenced by a winding path. On passing a piece of water called Sty Head Tarn, the bold and lofty crag of Great End appears on the left; and beyond it, in towering majesty, the highest of the Pikes, rendered more conspicuous by an object lately erected in the prosecution of the Trigonometrical Survey. Great Gable is close upon the right; but the grandeur of its form is better appreciated at a distance. The highest part of the road at Sty Head is 1250 feet above the nearest house; and in the first part of the descent, a magnificent view presents itself: the small valley of Wasdale Head appearing as if sunk below the general level, and the sea at a distance seeming to rise in the horizon. The lake of Wast Water is ñot yet in sight, being hid by a projecting mountain on the left, called Lingmell. A steep zigzag track now descends on the side of Gable, down which the horses may be led; as it is neither quite safe nor agreeable to ride. Crags of the most grotesque forms overlook the road, and the side of the hill is profusely strewed with stones, in some of which garnets may be found imbedded; and, in crossing the stream which issues between Gable and Kirkfell, a rock of reddish granite may be seen in the bed of the rivulet.

Wasdale Head comprises a level area of 400 acres of land, divided by stone walls into small irregular fields, which have been cleared with great industry and labour; as appears from the enormous heaps of stones, piled up from the surplus after completing the inclosures. Here six or seven families have their Chapel, of a size proportionate to the number of inhabitants, and in a style according with the situation; and what Mr. Gray formerly said of Grasmere, may with equal propriety be applied to this vale: "Not a single red tile, no gentleman's flaring house, or garden walls, break in upon the repose of this little unsuspected para-

dise; but all is peace, rusticity, and happy poverty,
in its neatest, most becoming attire."

After passing the inhabited part of the valley,
the road approaches the lake, which shews the
purity of its water, by the clean blue gravel washed
upon its shores.   As the road proceeds along the
margin of the lake, the screes on the opposite side
form a striking object, and the mountains left behind should not be forgotten; retrospective views
taken at short intervals, will shew the majestic and
varied forms they assume, on being viewed from
different points.   After passing Over Beck Bridge
at the foot of Bowderdale, and just before entering
the gate, the mountain Yewbarrow appears in a
fine conical shape, and between the slopes of it
and Lingmel, the distance is beautifully filled up

HEAD OF WAST WATER.

by Gable; and one of the best views of the lake is
a mile further on, from a rocky projecting knoll;
or from the grounds of Wasdale Hall.

It has been suggested, that Wast Water would
be more advantageously seen, by reversing the
excursion, so that the principal mountain views
would be always in prospect on advancing up the

vale. As far as relates to Wast Water alone, this
is certainly true; but in what concerns Borrowdale,
Lowes Water, and Crummock, they are seen to
more advantage by this route; besides, tourists
generally congratulate themselves on having passed
over the most difficult part of the road on the
first day.

Towards the lower parts of the lake, the shores
are more rocky; and the composition of the rock
is changed, from a kind of greenstone, to a reddish
sienite.

Having left the lake about a mile, a road turns
off on the left to Ravenglass; and at the Strands,
near the Church of Nether Wasdale, there are
two small public houses, at one of which it may
be necessary to take some refreshment, after a
morning's ride of 20 miles, and none of the best
road.

About four miles further, is the village of Gosforth, where a tall column, carved with unintel-
ligible characters, stands in the church-yard on the
right; beyond which the roads from Wasdale, Eskdale and Ravenglass become united. The country
now becomes more cultivated, and the principal
views are towards the sea, with the Isle of Man in
the distance; and the mountain rocks are succeeded by a red sandstone. From hence it is
nearly three miles of excellent road to Calder
Bridge, at which place are two neat small inns,
where lodgings are generally taken for the night.
Three quarters of a mile above the bridge, lie the

remains of Calder Abbey, mentioned at p. 79, to which it is a pleasant walk. The path leads by the side of the river Calder, where its banks are finely covered with wood; and passing the mansion of T. Irwin, Esq., which adjoins the Abbey, the venerable ruin appears to the view. Ponsonby Hall, the residence of E. Stanley, Esq., M. P., is at a short distance from the bridge; and the parish Church stands in the park. Captain Irwin has built and endowed a neat Chapel in the village of Calder Bridge, which stands in the parish of St. Bridget's, Beckermont.

### RETURN FROM CALDER BRIDGE TO KESWICK.

| MILES. | | MILES. |
|---|---|---|
| 7 | Ennerdale Bridge... ..................... | 7 |
| 3 | Lamplugh Cross ........................ | 10 |
| 4 | Lowes Water ........................... | 14 |
| 2 | Scale Hill ............................. | 16 |
| 4 | Buttermere ............................ | 20 |
| 9 | Keswick ...... ........................ | 29 |

From Calder Bridge there is an excellent road of ten miles to Whitehaven; but that usually taken by tourists, on horseback or on foot, inclines more towards the mountains; which, however, on this side present no very interesting features. For some miles the principal prospect is over a culti- vated country to the sea, with the Isle of Man and the Scotch mountains in the distance.

About three miles from Calder Bridge, the two rival points of Scawfell appear over the neigh- bouring mountains, separated by the yawning chasm of Mickle Door; and two miles further, the town of Egremont is seen through a narrow vale on the left. Seven miles from Calder Bridge, a part of Ennerdale Lake appears in sight; and after passing the hamlet of Ennerdale Bridge, in which stand the church and two small public-houses, the lake is observed from the rising ground in another point of view, accompanied by the grand mountain scenery of Ennerdale, amid which the Pillar rises conspicuous.

Turning to the right, by the public-house at Lamplugh Cross, in a mile further you pass between the hall and the church: the hall is now rebuilt in the shape of a modern farm-house, the only remains of its ancient grandeur being a gateway, with the inscription, "John Lamplugh, 1595." Two miles further, turning to the right at the farm-house called Fangs, and descending the hill, we first come in sight of the small lake of Lowes Water, accompanied by a rich assemblage of mountains. On the left, beyond Low Fell, we have the towering, barren front of Grasmoor, succeeded by Whiteless Pike, Robinson, and Rannerdale Knot, beyond Crummock Lake. On the right lie Burnbank and Carling Knot; in front, Melbreak rises in an aspiring cone, flanked by High Stile and Red Pike on one hand, and the peaked, perpendicular front of Honister Crag on the other. Between the last and Rannerdale Knot is just seen a part of the mountain called Hay Stacks, near Stonethwaite, in Borrowdale;

at a gate opening to the common, the top of the Pillar may be seen to the right of Red Pike. Soon after passing this lake, that of Crummock presents itself in one of its best combinations: the mountains seeming to have changed places since we viewed them on Lowes Water. Then crossing the river Cocker, you shortly arrive at Scale Hill, distant from Calder Bridge rather more than 16 miles.

If Buttermere has not been previously visited, a boat may be taken upon Crummock Lake, which, with a walk from the edge of the water to Scale Force, will make a pleasing variety. In the meantime the horses may meet the party at Buttermere, and the return to Keswick be made through Newlands—making this day's journey nearly 30 miles. Those who have seen Buttermere, may save above a mile, by taking the carriage road from Scale Hill: along which there is a pleasant view of the vale of Lorton; and also a fine view of the vale of Keswick in descending the hill from Whinlatter. Those who think this circuit too much for two days, may extend it to three, by staying one night at Nether Wasdale, and another at Scale Hill.

To visit Wast Water in a carriage from Keswick, it will be necessary to go by Scale Hill, Lowes Water, and Lamplugh, and by Ennerdale Bridge and over Cold Fell, or by Egremont, to Calder Bridge; thence to the Strands and Wast Water. At Strands a boat may be procured; and, if desired, Scawfell Pike may be ascended: and after stopping one or two nights at Calder Bridge, the return may be by Egremont, Cleator, and Lamplugh, or by Whitehaven.

DRIVE ROUND BASSENTHWAITE LAKE.

| MILES. | | MILES. |
|---|---|---|
| 8 | Peel-Wyke | 8 |
| 1 | Ouse Bridge | 9 |
| 1 | Castle Inn | 10 |
| 3 | Bassenthwaite Sandbed | 13 |
| 5 | Keswick | 18 |

This being thought less interesting than most of the other lakes, is often reserved to the last; but some have remarked that it ought to be visited first, or before the imagination became too much elated by the more prominent features of the other lakes. However, tourists who prefer an easy journey, will find objects to please, in a perambulation of 18 miles round this lake. On the western side the road is much improved, and rendered very commodious for travelling; it is in some parts enclosed in woods, in others opening to excellent views. There is a public-house at Peel-Wyke on the western side, another at Castle Inn on the eastern. The road at the foot of the lake is much encumbered by trees; but by walking a few paces through a gate, nearly opposite Armathwaite Hall, the prospect from the margin of the lake is extensive; and the botanist may perhaps find something worth his notice. On the eastern side, the traveller would sometimes wish for a nearer approach to the lake; but few would think themselves

N 2

repaid for the trouble of visiting West's stations on the promontories of Broadness and Scarness.

Those who are not inclined to make the whole circuit of the lake, may take a ride by the foot of Skiddaw, to a station a little above the road upon an open common, at the distance of five miles from Keswick. Here the principal part of the lake may be seen, with the three bold promontories of Bowness, Broadness, and Scarness, and in returning (if on horseback or on foot) take the upper road, by Millbeck, Applethwaite, and Ormathwaite, from whence some of the best views of Derwent Lake and its environs will be found. From Applethwaite, or Ormathwaite, they may take the nearest road to Keswick, or proceed by an occupation way along the side of Latrigg, and enter the town by the Penrith road.

### KESWICK TO ULLSWATER.

| MILES. | | MILES. |
|---|---|---|
| 8 | Moor End | 8 |
| 7 | Gowbarrow Park | 15 |
| 5 | Patterdale | 20 |
| | *Return the same way, or* | |
| 10 | Pooley Bridge | 30 |
| 6 | Penrith | 36 |

Ullswater may be visited from Keswick on horseback or on foot; leaving the Penrith road at the third mile-stone, crossing the vale of Wanthwaite, and passing over a bleak mountain side to Matterdale. Carriages have formerly been obliged to continue on the turnpike road to Beckses, eleven miles; but a new road is now constructed on the western side of Mell Fell, which shortens the distance two miles. After leaving St. John's Vale and the mountain Saddleback behind, these roads are equally uninteresting, till they unite at Dockray; but after entering Gowbarrow Park, the prospect of Ullswater is presented in one of its richest points of view; exhibiting the upper reach of the lake, with its three islands and delightful bays. Place Fell in front, rising immediately from the water's edge to the height of 1160 feet, and to the right a vast assemblage of mountains; among which Scandale Fell and Saint Sunday Crag rise conspicuous. Airey Force and Lyulph's Tower lie a little to the left, and it is then between four and five miles of delightful road to the inn at Patterdale, or six to Pooley Bridge. It has been customary for carriages from Keswick to be taken by Dacre to Pooley Bridge; but a preferable route is to turn off just beyond Penruddock, and cross the valley to Bennet Head; by which a much earlier and better view of Ullswater is obtained before reaching the inn.

An attempt to enumerate all the permutations that might be made in these excursions; or all the pleasing points, from which the varied scenery of this interesting region might be viewed; would be an endless, and, in fact, an useless task. Persons who delight in exploring a country, need only be made acquainted with the outlines: they will feel more pleasure in finding out the rest.

As an Appendix to these directions, it may not
be irrelevant to mention some objects which may
be seen on the way, to and from the lakes, by different lines of road; for which the author is partly
indebted to the *Penny Magazine.*

Returning from the lakes, by way of Kendal
towards Leeds, the tourist crosses the vale of
Lune, at Kirkby Lonsdale.  Near Ingleton, the
mountain Ingleborough, the waterfall of Thornton
Force, and the Slate Quarries, are interesting to
the geologist as well as to the lover of the picturesque: also the caves of Yordas and Weathercote, with others of smaller note; at the foot of
a steep hill, a mile before reaching Settle, by the
side of the road, is the celebrated ebbing and flowing well of Giggleswick.  Four miles to the east
of Settle, lie Malham Cove and Gordale Scar,
two of the most remarkable spots in England.
Wharfdale, still more to the east, is beautiful from
its source in the moors, to Otley and Harewood,
a few miles from Leeds.  The grounds of Bolton
Abbey are the gem of this valley.

From Penrith, the eastern road by Stainmoor
and Leeminglane skirts a lovely country.  There
is some pretty scenery between Penrith and Appleby, and the wild road over Stainmoor is striking and pleasant on a fine day.  From Bowes,
Barnard Castle may be visited; and Teesdale, one
of the finest Yorkshire valleys, with its two waterfalls, High Force and Cauldron Snout; also Winch

Bridge, one of the first attempts at a bridge of suspension.

At Greta Bridge, on the high road, lies the well-known scenery of Rokeby. At Catterick Bridge the Swale is crossed, about three miles below Richmond. Swaledale has some pretty scenery, but is inferior to Wensleydale, the next valley to the south, which is traversed by the Ure, and extends westward nearly to Ingleborough. Hardraw Scar, near Hawes, Aysgarth Force, near Askrigg, and Jeveraux Abbey are the most remarkable objects in it. Lower down, on the banks of the Ure, near Ripon, stands Fountains Abbey, which needs no praise. Ripon Minster is a fine specimen of our early ecclesiastical architecture. From Ripon there is a double communication with the south, either by Boroughbridge and the York road; or by Harrogate, Harewood, and Leeds. Knaresborough possesses some objects of curiosity, but scarcely sufficient to lead the tourist so far out of his way.

A party from Kendal might visit the scenery of Wensleydale by going first to Sedbergh, and thence through the vale of Garsdale to Hawes; or having proceeded as far as Ingleton, after viewing the natural curiosities in that neighbourhood, may go from thence to Askrigg, and there fall into the route above described.

# BOTANICAL NOTICES.

----

THE author will not here attempt a systematic arrangement of the botany of the district, nor even an enumeration of all the rare plants that may be met with, in a region possessing such variety of soil and situation—but merely, a brief notice of some of those which not unfrequently present themselves to the observation of the tourist, without going far out of his way to seek them.

In shallow parts of Lakes, where the bottom is of peat, the *Scirpus lacustris* and *Arundo Phragmitis*,* Bull-Rush and Common Reed, rear their heads on high above the water; the leaves and flowers of the *Nymphæ alba* and *Nuphar lutea*, the White and the Yellow Water-Lily, float upon the surface; and the bottom is rendered verdant by a commixture of *Lobelia Dortamanna, Littorella lacustris*, and *Isoetes lacustris*. The *Lobelia* spreads a tuft of radical leaves upon the bottom, and in July shoots up its spike of delicate pale flowers above the water; the *Littorella* puts forth its long and slender stamina most freely, when in

----

* The *Arundo Phragmitis*, said by authors to blossom in **July**, does not blow here before the latter end of September.

a dry summer it is left uncovered upon the shore; and the *Isoetes*, being one of the plants which perfect their fructification under water, has its leaves pulled up by water-fowl, in the winter season, to extract the seeds which lie concealed in their bases.

Several species of *Potamogeton*, Pond-weed, grow in the lakes. *Myriophyllum spicatum* and *Sium inundatum* inhabit slow streams and shallow parts of lakes. *Chara flexilis* grows in shallow, and *C. vulgaris* in deeper parts of Derwent Lake. *Sparganium ramosum*, in ditches; *S. natans*, in Derwent Lake: both of these, with *S. simplex*, may be found in Naddle-beck, near Keswick. *Typha latifolia** also grows at the last-mentioned place; *T. angustifolia*, in Rydal Water.

The spongy shores of the lakes and pools are margined with *Equisetum limosum*; *Hippuris vulgaris* grows in ditches near Cartmel Well; *Cladium Mariscus*, on the edge of Cunswick Tarn, near Kendal; *Ranunculus aquatilis*, Water Crowfoot, in the rivers Derwent, Kent, and Eamont; *Œnanthe crocata*, in the river Brathay; *Myosotis palustris*, Water Scorpion-grass, or Forget-me-not, and *Alisma plantago*, Water-Plantain, are common; *Nasturtium officinale*, Water-cress, in springs and ditches, in calcareous soils, but has been rare among the lakes till increased by planting.

---

* This differs from the description given by Sir J. E. Smith, in the stem being leafy all the way up. It is, I believe, the *angustifolia* that has its leaves all from the bottom.

Meadows subject to lake floods are covered
with the various species of *Carex*, along with the
*Eriophorum angustifolium*, many-headed Cotton-
grass; *Eriophorum vaginatum*, the single-headed
Cotton-grass, on the boggy parts of mountains, is
called Moss-crops, and is the early spring food of
sheep; *Menyanthes trifoliata*, Buckbean, *Comarum
palustre*, *Juncus filiformis*, and *Juncus uliginosus*,
on the isthmus near Derwent Lake; the last
named, when on shore, is a low creeping plant,
but, rooted under water, it shoots up leaves like
hairs to the length of a foot or more.

*Saxifraga aizoides*, in watery places on Barrow
Side, near Keswick; *S. granulata*, in drier ground
near the same place, and at Mayburgh; *S. hyp-
noides*, near Thirlmere, Kirkstone, and Long
Sleddale; *S. stellaris*, near the summits of Skid-
daw and Helvellyn; *S. tridactylites*, at Keswick.
*Saxifraga oppositifolia* has been observed by H.
C. Watson, Esq., near Great End Crag, in Bor-
rowdale. *Chrysosplenium oppositifolium*, Golden
Saxifrage, is common on the margin of springs.

*Cochlearia officinalis*, Scurvy-grass, is abundant
in springs on both sides of Helvellyn, but rarely
found in other parts of the lake district. *Parnassia palustris*, Grass of Parnassus, and *Narthecium Ossifragum*, Bog Asphodel, in moist
elevated pastures on the way to Skiddaw. *Primula farinosa*, Bird's-eye, in similar situations,
in Loughrigg, near Bampton, Hesket Newmarket,
and Cunswick Tarn. *Pinguicula vulgaris*, But-

terwort, and *Drosera rotundifolia*, Sun-dew, common in shallow bogs; *D. longifolia* is more rare, but found in Borrowdale, and Ullock Moss, where the bog is deeper.

*Vaccinium Oxycoccos*, Cran-berry, grows in poor boggy ground, sparingly near Rydal Water, in Thornthwaite, and more plentifully in Mungrisdale; *V. Myrtillus*, Bilberry, Whortle-berry, or Blea-berry, is common in rocky woods and on mountain sides, near Derwent Lake and on Skiddaw Dod; *V. Vitis idæa*, Red Whortle-berry or Cow-berry, inhabits loftier situations, and retains its fruit longer: it grows on the summit of Skiddaw, but is more fruitful on the mountains between Derwent and Crummock Lakes. *Empetrum nigrum* grows at a great altitude upon mountains, in a moist soil; its berries are said to be the food of grouse. *Arbutus Uva-ursi*, found by Mr. Watson on the west side of Grasmoor, and *Silene acaulis* near Great-end Crag: the last is also found on Helvellyn and Fairfield.

Large tracts of peaty moors are covered with *Calluna vulgaris*, common Ling, which affords shelter for grouse; in August, its blossoms give the mountains a rich purple hue, and it is the source from which bees obtain a great portion of their honey: a variety is sometimes observed with white flowers. *Erica cinerea* grows in places more rocky, and remains longer in blossom; *E. Tetralix*, in Ullock Moss and Gosforth. *Statice Armeria*, Thrift, or Sea Gilliflower, in salt marshes, and near the top of Scawfell. *Rhodiola rosea*, and *Oxyria reniformis*, in the rocks of Helvellyn, Scawfell, Raven Scar, and Ashness Gill.

*Ulex europæus*, the large early flowering Furze or Whin, is too common in the neighbourhood of Keswick; *Ulex nanus*, a smaller kind, blossoming in autumn, is more prevalent between Pooley Bridge and Askham, in Buttermere, and Wasdale; at Bolton Wood, near Gosforth, intermixed with the large blossomed heath, it gives an appearance of richness to land otherwise barren. *Juniperus communis*, the common Juniper, erroneously called Savin, grows on the mountain between Wythburn and Borrowdale, on Place Fell, Loughrigg Fell, at a great altitude upon Grisedale Pike, and most plentifully in the pastures between Windermere and Coniston. *Salix herbacea*, the least Willow, on the summit of Skiddaw, on Saddleback, Helvellyn, and the mountains between Derwent and Crummock Lake. *Alchemilla alpina*, Cinquefoil Lady's Mantle, on the mountain between Borrowdale and Buttermere, and at the foot of Wanthwaite Crags.

*Orchis bifolia*, *O. maculata*, and *O. conopsea*, one to two miles from Keswick, on the Penrith road; the last on Hartley Hill, Buttermere. *Orchis mascula*, *Listera Ovata*, and *L. Nidus-Avis*, under Wallow Crag; *L. Cordata*, near Helvellyn. *Erythræa Centaurium*, *Gentiana campestris*, *Cynoglossum officinale*, *Erodium cicutarium*, and *Geranium sanguineum*, near Flimby; *Agrimonia Eupato-*

*ria, Campanula latifolia, Geranium sylvaticum* and *G. pratense, Lysimachia vulgaris, Rosa cinnamomia,* and *Senecio saracenicus,* in Howray, near Keswick; *Campanula glomerata,* near Ullswater. *Meum athamanticum,* Spignel, Bristow Hills, near Keswick; *Peucedanum Ostruthium,* in Legberthwaite; *Lepidium hirtum,* Crow Park, near Keswick; *Thalictrum majus?* and *Genista tinctoria,* at the foot of Bassenthwaite.

*Pimpinella Saxifraga,* Burnet Saxifrage, and *Sanguisorba officinalis,* Great Burnet, are common in the fields; *Poterium Sanguisorba,* Salad Burnet, on Kirkhead in Cartmel, and on Kendal Fell; *Primula Veris,* Cowslip, is common in calcareous soils, but rarely found among the lakes. *Chrysanthemum segetum,* the Yellow Corn Marigold, was formerly so troublesome in some corn fields, that the land infested with it was considered inferior in value; but by the improved system of husbandry it is nearly eradicated. *Chrysanthemum Leucanthemum,* the Great Daisy, in grass lands, is increasing in an extraordinary manner in many parts of the lake district: *Pyrethrum inodorum* is a troublesome weed near the sea coast.

When land has been exhausted by continuing too long under tillage, it is subject to be overrun by *Potentilla anserina,* White Tansey or Silverweed, *Tussilago Farfara,* Colt's-foot, and *Holcus mollis;* which last appears to be the natural Couchgrass or Twitch of the district; *Triticum repens* is sometimes introduced among other seeds.

The rare *Pyrola secunda* and *P. media?** have been found among the rocks near Keswick; *P. minor? Impatiens Noli-me-tangere, Hypericum Androsæmum,* and *Arum maculatum,* near Ambleside; *Eupatorium cannabinum,* near Low Wood Inn, and in Wasdale; *Bidens tripartita,* near Keswick. *Convallaria majalis,* Lily of the Valley, on an island in Windermere, and near Skelwith Force; *Anchusa sempervirens,* at Bowness and Long Sleddale; *Paris quadrifolia,* One-berry, on the turnpike side near Bannerigg, in a lane between Elleray and Bowness, and in Lowther woods. *Tamus communis,* Bryony or Wild Vine, with its red berries, ornaments the hedges near Windermere lake, but is rarely found further north. *Vicia sylvatica,* on the banks of the Lune, and *Saponaria officinalis* under the bridge at Kirkby Lonsdale; *Origanum vulgare,* at Kirkby Lonsdale, Humphrey Head, and Mayburgh; *Parietaria officinalis,* Wall Pelitory, near Cartmel Well, and on the walls of Cartmel Church. *Meconopsis cambrica,* Yellow Poppy, in Long Sleddale; *Glaucium luteum,* Yellow Horned-poppy, on the coast near Maryport and Flookburgh; *Hyoscyamus niger,* Henbane, near the last place; *Atropa Beladonna* has also been found there, and about Furness Abbey. *Geranium pratense, Malva moschata,* and *Campanula latifolia,* about Kirkby Lonsdale.

---

* A note of interrogation signifies some doubt as to the species.

Many of the plants inhabiting woody ground may be found in Castlehead Wood, near Keswick; such are *Anemone nemorosa, Asperula odorata, Betonica officinalis, Circæa lutetiana, Convallaria multiflora, Corydalis claviculata, Digitalis purpurea, Epilobium montanum, Erysimum Alliaria, Geranium lucidum, G. robertianum, Geum urbanum, Hyacinthus non scriptus, Hypericum pulchrum, H. perforatum, Lapsana communis, Lychnis dioica, Lysimachia Nemorum, Melampyrum pratense, Mercurialis perennis, Orobus tuberosus, Oxalis acetosella, Prenanthes muralis, Primula vulgaris, Sanicula europæa, Scorphularia nodosa, Stellaria holostea, S. graminea, Tormentilla officinalis, Teucrium Scorodonia, Veronica Chamædrys*, and *V. officinalis.*

Upon the rocky summit grow *Alchemilla arvensis, Capsella Bursa-pastoris, Cerastium vulgatum, C. viscosum, Draba verna, Galium cruciatum, G. verum Geranium dissectum, G. molle, Jasione montanum, Myosostis versicolor,*[*] *Rosa spinosissima, Rumex Acetosa, R. Acetosella, Sedum Telephium, S. Anglicum,*[†] *Sisymbrium thalianum, Teesdalia nudicaulis, Thymus Serpyllum, Veronica arvensis, V. serpyllifolia.*

In the moist ground at its foot: *Angelica sylvestris, Chrysosplenium oppositifolium, Epilobium tetragonum, Equisetum limosum, Spiræa, Ulmaria*, and *Valeriana officinalis.*

---

[*] Blossom yellow at first, and turning blue.
[†] Introduced from Loughrigg Fell in 1833.

Between the road to Lowdore and the edge of Derwent lake: *Achillæa Millefolium, A. Ptarmica, Antirrhinum Linaria, Cardamine amara, Circæa alpina, Galium boreale, Hydrocotyle vulgaris, Hypericum Elodes, Lythrum salicaria, Myrica, Gale, Lotus Corniculatus, Narthecium ossifragum, Œnanthe crocata,* Orchis mascula, O. maculata, Parnassia palustris, Silene maritima, Thalictrum majus? Trollius europæus, Vaccinium Myrtillus, V. Oxycoccos, Valeriana dioica,* and *Valeriana officinalis.*

Ullock Moss, near Keswick, produces *Calluna vulgaris, Comarum palustre, Drosera rotundifolia, D. longifolia, Eleocharis cæspitosa, Eriophorum angustifolium, E. vaginatum, Erica Tetralix, Hypericum Elodes, Melica cærulea, Myrica Gale, Osmunda regalis, Rhamnus Frangula, Rhynchospora alba, Scutellaria galericulata, Utricularia minor,* and *Veronica scutellata.*

In a bog behind the inn at Patterdale may be found, *Anagallis tenella, Parnassia palustris, Drosera rotundifolia, Pinguicula vulgaris, Menyanthes trifoliata,* and *Sphagnum palustris.*

Near a place called Scroggs, in Loughrigg, and chiefly in a small pasture called the Old Close, among óther more common plants, may be found the following: *Alchemilla vulgaris, Aquilegia vulgaris, Anagallis tenella, Arum maculatum, Chrysosplenium oppositifolium, Circæa lutetiana,*

---

* Without yellow juice, ~~perhaps the epifolia~~

*Drosera rotundifolia, Eriophorum angustifolium?*
*Geum urbanum, Hydrocotyle vulgaris, Hypericum*
*Androsæmum, H. pulchrum, H. quadrangulum,*
*Listera ovata, Lysimachia nemorum, Linum ca-*
*tharticum, Narthecium ossifragum, Orchis bifolia,*
*O. conopsea, O. mascula, O. maculata, Osmunda*
*regalis, Oxalis Acetosella, Primula farinosa, Par-*
*nassia palustris, Pedicularis palustris, P. sylvatica,*
*Pimpinella saxifraga, Pinguicula vulgaris, Poly-*
*podium Phegopteris, Saxifraga aizoides, Sedum*
*anglicum, S. Telephium, Tormentilla officinalis,*
*Teucrium Scorodonia,* and *Thymus Serpyllum.*

Many species of lichens may be found upon the
rocks, and on the trees; mosses upon the mountains and heaths; and ferns, upon the commons
and in the woods. *Lycopodium clavatum,* Club-
moss, Stag's-horn-moss, Fox-feet, or Wolf's-claw,
grows upon dry mountains not very high; *L. al-*
*pinum,* in more lofty; *L. Selago,* in lofty and
more moist places, and *L. Selaginoides* by the
edges of rills.

The sides of mountains with a dry soil are
clothed to a moderate elevation with *Pteris aqui-*
*lina,* Brackens, which, by their changing in September and October from a bright to an olive
green, and afterwards to a russet brown, contribute to that autumnal colouring which is so much
admired. *Cryptogramma crispa,* Stone fern, inhabits higher and more rocky situations.

On the road between Kendal and Bowness are
found, *Aspidium Filix-mas, Asplenium Adiantum-*

*nigrum*, *A. Filix-fœmina*, *A. Trichomanes*, *Cistoptris fragilis*, *Cryptogramma crispa*, *Polypodium Dryopteris*, *P. vulgaris*, and *Pteris aquilina*.

*Scolopendrium vulgare*, in rents in limestone rocks in Westmorland, and at Calder Bridge. *Grammitis Ceterach*, *Asplenium ruta-muraria*, and *A. Trichomanes*, on Troutbeck Bridge; *A. viride*, in Ashness Gill; *A. ruta-muraria*, at Lairbeck, and Hill-top, near Keswick; *Hymenophyllum Wilsoni*, at foot of Lowdore fall, at Dungeon Gill, and Scale Force; *Polypodium Phegopteris*, at Scale Force, Wythburn, and Patterdale; *Osmunda regalis*, at Skelwith, and in the Cass, near Keswick.

In a walk round Castlehead and Cockshot, near Keswick, may be seen *Polypodium vulgaris*, *P. Dryopteris*, *Aspidium Filix-mas*, *A. Oreopteris*, *A. dilatatum*, *Asplenium Adiantum-nigrum*, *A. Filix-fœmina*, *A. Trichomanes*, and *Blechnum boreale*, and on Barrow Common, *Botrychium*, *Lunaria*, and *Ophioglossum vulgatum*, have sometimes been found.

*Rhamnus frangula*, Berry-bearing Alder, in Graithwaite woods, near Rydal Water, in Cockshot Wood, and the Cass, near Keswick: *Ligustrum vulgare*, Privet, and *Cratœgus Aria*, White-beam, grow on the rocks at Humphrey Head; *Euonymus europœus*, on Barrow-side, near Lowdore.

The Oak, Ash, and Birch are the principal indigenous forest trees. Sycamores have formerly been planted round homesteads, and make an excellent shelter; withstanding cold blasts and sea breezes better than almost any other tree. Extensive plantations of Larches have been made within the last fifty years, but do not add much beauty to the country; and they are gradually giving way to the monarch of the forest, the English Oak. The Hawthorn attains a great size on the banks of Ullswater; much of the underwood is of Hasel, producing, especially in Borrowdale, large quantities of nuts; which, however, of late years, probably on account of the coldness of the spring seasons, have been less plentiful than formerly.

Stunted Yew trees creep up the perpendicular escarpments of the limestone rocks near Humphrey Head, Witherslack, and Underbarrow.

> "—— But worthier still of note
> Are those fraternal four of Borrowdale,
> Join'd in one solemn and capacious grove."

The bole of one of these, near the Black-lead mine, is twenty feet in circumference, and its branches cover an area of twenty yards diameter:

> "Produced too slowly ever to decay,
> Of form and aspect too magnificent
> To be destroyed."

One in Lorton Vale is still more umbrageous,

> "Which to this day stands single in the midst
> Of its own darkness, as it stood of yore."
>
> WORDSWORTH.

# THE GEOLOGY

OF THE

## LAKE DISTRICT.

———

WHEN this essay was first published, in 1820, the structure of the mountainous district of Cumberland, Westmorland, and Lancashire, was but little understood; scientific travellers had contented themselves with procuring specimens of the different rocks, without taking time to become acquainted with their relative position. Since that time, the subject has received more attention from persons conversant with geological inquiries: especially from the distinguished Professor Sedgwick, who, in 1821 and following years, subjected this district to his untiring examination. In his address to the Geological Society, Feb. 18th, 1831, the Rev. Professor deigned to compliment the author as being the first to point out that "the greater part of the central region of the Lake Mountains is occupied by three distinct groups of stratified rocks of a slaty texture."

Notwithstanding all that may have been said or written upon the subject, the following remarks may still be acceptable to such as require only a general outline; and to those who feel disposed to explore for themselves, the facts here stated may be useful, in directing them more readily to the objects of their research.

In entering upon a geological description of this district, the granite, occupying the lowest place in the known series of rocks, forms a convenient starting place, from whence it seems most natural, though contrary to the practice of modern geologists, to proceed in the *ascending* order.

What has been the condition of granite before the deposition of the matter of incumbent rocks, may be left to conjecture; that portions of it have been subsequently protruded through them, is now generally admitted. It does not, however, in this district, reach the summit of any of the principal mountains; it is exposed to view in some of their ravines, and in places where it forms hills or ridges, they are of moderate elevation.

A rock of granite, composed of quartz, white felspar, and black mica, may be seen denudated in the bed of the river Caldew, on the north-east side of Skiddaw; and in a branch of the river Greta, between Skiddaw and Saddleback, about 1400 feet above the level of the sea. It is traversed in various directions by veins of quartz; in some of which, molybdena, apatite, tungsten, wolfram, and other minerals have been found.

A variety of granite with reddish felspar, and which, from a deficiency of mica, has sometimes been called sienite, forms two inferior mountain ridges, called Irton Fell and Muncaster Fell: it extends to some distance on both sides of the river Esk, and may be seen shooting up in places, almost as far as Bootle, and also at Wasdale Head. At Netherwasdale it becomes a finer grained sienite, in which form it extends through the mountains quite across Ennerdale, as far as Scale Force, and to the side of Buttermere Lake. It contains veins of red hematite and micaceous iron ore. Another variety of granite with reddish felspar in large crystallized masses, is found on Shap Fells, and may be observed *in situ* on the road side near Wasdale Bridge, about four miles south of Shap.

Carrock Fell consists of a rock generally classed with the sienites, but varying in appearance in different parts of the mountain. It contains (besides the usual ingredients of quartz and felspar) hypersthene and magnetic or titaniferous iron ore in various proportions. Near this, a considerable quantity of lead ore and some copper has been procured: the lead, being smelted and refined, yields a good portion of silver.

A reddish porphyritic rock occurs on both sides of St. John's Vale, from two to three miles east of Keswick; and a vein or dyke apparently related to the same, but far more beautiful, (being composed of crystals of quartz and bright red felspar, imbedded in a brownish red compact felspar,) is found on Armboth Fell, and is partially exposed on the Ambleside road, near the seven mile stone from Keswick.

The rocks constituting the greatest bulk of the Lake Mountains have been commonly described under the general appellation of slate, although many of them shew no disposition to the slaty cleavage. They may be divided into three groups, which have been, in a former edition, called the Clayslate, Greenstone, and Greywacké divisions; the last of which seems now to belong to, or be included in, what Mr. Murchison calls the Silurian System.

Of these divisions, the FIRST, or Clayslate, being lowest in the series, forms Skiddaw, Saddleback, Grasmoor, and Grisedale Pike, with the mountains of Thornthwaite and Newlands; it extends across Crummock Lake, and by the foot of Ennerdale, as far as Dent Hill; and after being lost for several miles, it is elevated again at Black Comb.

If we regard the granite of Skiddaw as a nucleus upon which these rocks are deposited in mantle-shaped strata, that which reposes immediately upon it is commonly called gneiss; but being rather more slaty, and less granular, than the gneiss of some other countries, it is sometimes called mica slate. More distant from the granite, the quantity of mica is diminished, and the slate is marked with darker coloured spots; it is then provincially called Whintin, and is quarried for flooring-flags and other useful purposes. This again is succeeded by a slate of a softer kind, in

P

which crystals of chiastolite are plentifully imbedded: as we approach the summit of Skiddaw, these crystals gradually disappear, and it there becomes a more homogeneous clayslate.

These rocks are of a blackish colour, and divide by natural partings into slates of various thickness, which are sometimes curiously bent and waved: when these partings are very numerous, though indistinct at first, they open by exposure to the weather, and in time it becomes shivered into thin flakes, which lessens its value as a roofing slate. In some places, the thin laminæ alternate with others of a few inches in thickness; which are harder, and of a lighter colour, containing more siliceous matter; and, from the sonorous quality of some of those slates, a set reduced to a musical scale has been for half a century exhibited at Crosthwaite's Museum, in Keswick. More recently, sets, extended to a greater compass, have been exhibited in London, Liverpool, and other places with great success.

Rocks of this description have sometimes been represented as stratified, and the strata parallel to the slaty cleavage; but this proposition should not be received without some hesitation. If it be supposed that these varieties of rock, between which there is no natural parting, have been deposited in the order in which they have been mentioned; then, the strata may be said to be mantle-shaped round the granitic nucleus; only interrupted in continuity by the anomalous rocks of Carrock;

but if it be assumed that the stratification follows
the slaty cleavage, then it may be said to have its
bearing tending towards the north-east and south-
west; dipping generally at a high angle to the
south-east, and presenting the edges of its laminæ
to the surface of the granite, from the proximity
of which the nature and appearance of the rock
must be presumed to be altered.

The rocks belonging to this division do not effervesce with acids; they contain no calcareous
spar, except a little in some of the veins.   They
are sometimes intersected by dykes of a harder
kind of rock, apparently of the nature of trap or
greenstone.   Veins of lead ore occur in several
places; and have been worked between Skiddaw
and Saddleback, in Thornthwaite, Newlands, and
Buttermere: one in the parish of Loweswater, opposite the inn at Scale-hill, and one below the level
of Derwent Lake, have at times been the most
productive.   A copper mine had formerly been
worked to a great depth in a hill called Gold
Scalp, in Newlands, and is said to have produced
a very rich ore, which appears to have been the
yellow sulphuret, or copper pyrites.   A little cobalt
ore has formerly been got in Newlands, and small
quantities of manganese in various places.   A salt
spring, near the Grange, in Borrowdale, has anciently been in some repute for its medicinal qualities; another has been more recently discovered
in working a lead mine near Derwent Lake.   They

both issue from veins in this rock, but their source
remains unknown.

The SECOND, or Greenstone division, com-
prehends the mountains of Eskdale, Wasdale,
Ennerdale, Borrowdale, Langdale, Grasmere,
Patterdale, Martindale, Mardale, and some adjacent places; including the two highest mountains
of the district, Scawfell and Helvellyn, as well as
the Old Man at Coniston. All our fine towering
crags belong to it; and most of the cascades
among the lakes fall over it. There are indeed
some lofty precipices in the former division; but,
owing to the shivery and crumbling nature of the
rock, they present none of the bold colossal features which are exhibited in this.

Most of these rocks are of a pale-bluish or
grey colour; some are porphyritic, others of a
slaty structure; differing however from the slates
of the last division, inasmuch as these exhibit no
distinct partings by which they are to be separated.
A reddish aggregated rock, of a coarse slaty structure, is to be seen on entering the common on the
road from Keswick towards Borrowdale. It appears to form one of the lower beds of the division,
and may be traced each way to some distance. It
is succeeded by the compact dark-coloured rock of
Wallow Crag, in which quartz, calcareous spar,
chlorite, and epidote, are found in veins. Garnets
are found imbedded in some of the rocks on Castlerigg Fell and Great Gable. An amygdaloid
rock, containing nodules of calcareous spar, and

sometimes of agate, opal, or calcedony, is met with in several places—as near Honister Crag—between Bowder Stone and Rosthwaite—on Castlerigg Fell, near Keswick—and in Wolf Crag, on the road to Matterdale. A curious mixed rock, of basaltic appearance, is found near Berrier; it skirts the north side of Caldbeck Fells, forms the hill called Binsey, and may be seen on the north side of the Derwent, near to Cockermouth.

The fine pale-blue roofing slate occurs in beds (called by the workmen, veins): the most natural position of the cleavage or bate of the slate appears to be vertical; but it is to be found in various degrees of inclination, both with respect to the horizon, and the planes of stratification. The direction of the slaty cleavage bears most commonly towards the north-east and south-west; while the dip or inclination is more variable: the former may be ascribed to some general operation of nature; the latter being influenced by local circumstances—such as the weight of a mountain pressing upon one side, while the other side is wanting a support. The direction and inclination of the strata are more distinguishable by stripes and alternations in the colour and texture, than by any natural partings; and the slates are split of various thickness, according to their fineness of grain, and the discretion and skill of the workman, without any previous indication of the place where they may be so divided. They do not separate into thin flakes, like those of the former division;

P 2

but some of them, when long used, are subject to a peculiar species of decay, which operates most powerfully on parts least exposed to the weather.

Most of the rocks of this division effervesce in some degree with acids, but more especially those possessing the slaty structure. They are not very productive of metallic ores, although they afford a considerable variety. A vein of lead ore has for some years been profitably worked at Greenside, in Patterdale; copper has formerly been got at Dalehead, in Newlands, which is near the northern boundary of the division—it consists of grey and purple copper, with specimens of malachite. A mine at Coniston, near the southern boundary, produces the yellow sulphuret; and a vein of the same was a few years ago opened at Wythburn. Small veins of iron ore are frequently met with, but scarcely thought worth notice. The famous plumbago, or black-lead mine of Borrowdale, is also situated in this division: but no organic remains have been discovered in either this or the preceding.

The THIRD division, or Silurian group—forming only inferior elevations—commences with a bed of dark-blue transition limestone, containing here and there a few shells and madrepores, and alternating with a slaty rock of the same colour; the different layers of each being in some places several feet, in others only a few inches in thickness. This limestone crosses the river Duddon near Broughton; passing Broughton Mills, it runs in a north-

east direction through Torver, by the foot of the
Old Man mountain, and appears near Low Yewdale and Yew Tree. Here it makes a considerable slip to the eastward, after which it ranges past
the Tarns upon the hills above Borwick ground;
and stretching through Skelwith, it crosses the
head of Windermere near Low Wood Inn. Then
passing above Dovenest and Skelgill, it traverses
the vales of Troutbeck, Kentmere, and Long
Sleddale; crossing the two intervening mountains
in the direction of the roads which lead over them;
so that no relation can be discovered between the
direction of the valleys and that of the stratification. It dips to the south-east, while the cleavage
of the slate with which it is associated, frequently
inclines in an opposite direction.

Towards the south-east succeeds a series of rocks
of the same dark-blue colour, and principally of a
slaty structure, but accompanied in places with a
rock which breaks alike in all directions. This
last has supplied a great portion of the rounded
stones found in the beds of the rivers Kent and
Lune; thus furnishing materials for paving the
streets, and repairing the roads in the vicinity.

A rock of fine-grained sienite is observed near
the foot of Coniston Lake; and one containing a
portion of mica appears in Crosthwaite. The
strata seams are more distinct in this than in the
preceding division; but, like that, it is not marked
by any natural partings in the plane of cleavage.
A quarry one mile from Brathay, on the road to-

wards Hawkshead, yields excellent flags for floor-
ing; and they are manufactured into tombstones
with good effect, by Mr. Webster, of Kendal, and
Mr. Bromley, of Keswick. This quarry affords a
good example of the stratification (or, as some will
have it, rhomboidal crystallization) of these rocks.
The cleavage is here nearly perpendicular; and the
strata, being from one foot to five in thickness, dip
to the south-east at an angle of about thirty degrees.   In some districts in Yorkshire the layers
are so much diminished in thickness, that slates
and tables are formed in the plane of the stratification, instead of the cleavage; and this has
probably given rise to the notion of two distinct
cleavages crossing each other under a certain
angle.   Roofing slate (called black slate, to distinguish it from the blue of the second division) is
manufactured in large quantities in the district
between Ulverston and Broughton; which is well
situated for shipping either by the river Duddon
or by canal from Ulverston.

The preference given to the slates from certain
quarries as requiring less weight, for the covering
of a roof of given dimensions, depends not so much
upon the specific gravity (which varies at most
from 2749 to 2800, or one part in 55) as upon the
fineness of grain, which enables it to bear splitting
thinner.   All the rocks of this division effervesce
more or less with acids; they contain some calcareous spar and pyrites; but little metallic ore, except a small quantity of galena, with green and

yellow phosphate of lead, which has been got near Staveley; and some yellow copper ore in Skelwith.

Although little notice has hitherto been taken by authors of the difference between the roofing slates of these three divisions, yet a workman of moderate experience will readily distinguish them: and I have endeavoured so to describe the peculiarities of each, that those who may hereafter be engaged in examining similar districts may be better enabled to compare them.

A conglomerate, composed of rounded stones of various sizes, from the smallest gravel, to the weight of several pounds, held together by a ferruhinous, calcareous cement, forms a hill of a parabolic shape, about 1200 feet in height, called Mell Fell; and some lesser elevations extending to the foot of Ullswater. The pebbles are evidently fragments of older rocks, rounded by attrition, and must have been transported from some distance, apparently from the southward: but what became of the surplus when the hill was rounded to its present shape? This has been generally taken as a member of the old red sandstone formation, which is understood to pass under the adjacent limestone, but, except perhaps near Shap Abbey, their actual contact or order of superposition has scarcely, in this district, been discovered.

A large mass of similar composition appears in the bed, and on the banks of the river Lune, at

Kirkby Lonsdale.   Its dip indicates that it should pass under the limestone which appears at a little distance; but its containing nodules of limestone seems to militate against this assumption,* except it can be supposed that the lower bed of limestone, which extends from Coniston through Long Sleddale, has been disrupted by the protrusion of the granite of Shap Fells; and the rounded fragments along with those of adjoining rocks, deposited here; and then, by going a step further, may many of the pebbles of Mell Fell be supposed to be derived from the same neighbourhood.   Something of the same kind also appears in the river Mint, from two to three miles above Kendal; where it may be seen to rest upon the blue rock; and wherever the subjacent rock can be seen, it is always deeply coloured by the iron of the conglomerate.   A layer of similar appearance is interstratified with the red sandstone at Barrow Mouth near Whitehaven; and a still newer formation of the same kind adjoins the Cartmel sands near Humphrey Head.

A superincumbent bed called the mountain, or upper transition limestone, mantles round these mountains, in a position unconformable to the strata of the slaty and other rocks upon which it reposes.   It bassets out near Egremont, Lamplugh, Pardshaw, Papcastle, Bothel, Ireby, Caldbeck, Hesket, Berrier, Dacre, Lowther, and Shap; it appears again near Kendal, Witherslack, Cart-

---

* A likely place for the decision of this question is in the bed of a brook in Casterton Wood.

mel, Dalton, and Millum, from whence for some distance its place is occupied by the sea; and in the neighbourhood of Gosforth and Calder Bridge, a red sandstone intervenes, so that the limestone is either wanting or buried under more recent formations. It dips from the mountains on every side, but with different degrees of inclination; the declivity being generally least on the southern side. In the neighbourhood of Witherslack it forms lofty isolated ridges, while the subjacent slaty rock appears in the lower ground; and it may be seen upon the surface as far as Warton and Farleton Crags, and even as far as Kellet, before it is covered by the sandstone of the coal measures. A remarkable exception, however, occurs in Holker Park, where the mountain rock is succeeded by limestone, and that by sandstone and shale, resembling that which accompanies coal—all within a very short distance. On the north and west of the mountains, the inclination of the newer rocks appears to be greater and the strata thinner; so that the clay-slate of the first division is succeeded by limestone, sandstone, and coal, all in the distance of two or three miles. The principal mineral production of this limestone, is iron ore, which is raised in great quantities near Dalton, and also near Egremont.

Beyond the circumference of the limestone district, various kinds of sandstone and coal succeed each other alternately; and a thin seam of coal has been found interstratified with the limestone at

Hesket Newmarket; but it is easily understood, that it would be in vain to look for coal within this limestone circle; consequently it cannot be found in the neighbourhood of the lakes. Coal is raised at Greysouthen, Gilcrux, and Plumbland; and there are extensive fields of coal beneath the town of Whitehaven; at Workington, and on the south side of the river Ellen at Maryport. From Maryport towards Carlisle, and thence to Penrith, is a large tract of red sandstone of unknown depth. To the eastward, the plain of the Eden is bounded by a long range of mountains, called by some the British Apennines, or the Back-bone of England. These mountains are stratified, but do not produce coal in any valuable quantity, except at the northern end towards Brampton. South-east, coal is found on Stainmoor; and more southward, its first appearance is near Hutton Roof, between Burton and Kirkby Lonsdale; and near Ingleton, there is an extraordinary assemblage of slate, lime, and coal.

Boulder stones are often met with, far removed from their native rock. They are often seen at a considerable elevation on the side of a valley opposite that from whence they have been produced; but do not appear to have been carried over high mountain ridges. The granite blocks from Shap Fells are scattered over a great part of Westmorland; but are not found in the neighbourhood of the lakes. Boulders from the sienite of Buttermere and Ennerdale are found on the west coast

of Cumberland; but not in the vales of Keswick
or Windermere. The granite of Caldew and
sienite of Carrock can be recognized in Boulders
in the neighbourhood of Carlisle; but are not seen
to the south of Keswick. The porphyritic Boulders from St. John's Vale, and the mountain east of
it, are frequent in the neighbourhood of Penrith;
the large stone in the centre of Mayburgh is of
that kind. The famous Bowder Stone of Borrowdale does not come within the present description; having apparently fallen from the adjacent
rock above; but a large block near Skelwith Bridge,
on the road to Grasmere—one near Coniston
Waterhead, and another near Gosforth, as well as
many others of smaller dimensions—are far more
interesting to the geologist; yielding sufficient
scope for conjecture as to the place of their origin,
and the mode of their removal.

Evidences of the operation of some extraordinary
power, at a former age of the world, may be observed in different valleys; especially those of
Borrowdale and Langdale, and also in the vicinity
of Windermere; where the surfaces of the lower
rocks are rounded and smoothed in a remarkable
manner. Some, who have become converts to a
recently promulgated theory, will attribute those
appearances to the agency of GLACIERS; but the
action of WATER seems more intelligible to the
mere English geologist.

# METEOROLOGY.

BESIDES the permanent beauties of a country diversified by hills and dales, mountains and lakes, there are transient subjects capable of arresting the attention of the contemplative observer; amongst which are,—the mists or fogs—forming over the surface of lakes—floating along the sides of hills —or collected into clouds, hovering upon the summits of mountains.

Mountains have been supposed to attract the clouds with which their summits are so frequently enveloped; but it is more to their agency in forming them, that the accumulation of clouds in mountainous countries may be attributed. Clouds are formed of aqueous particles floating in the atmosphere; and they serve as an awning, to shield the earth from the violence of the sun's rays in hot weather; and to protect it from the rigour of a cold winter's night, by obstructing the radiation of heat from its surface. In the clearest weather a portion of water always exists in the atmosphere in the state of an invisible vapour; and the higher the temperature, the greater quantity it is able to sustain; so that when air, fully saturated with

vapour, suffers a diminution of its heat, the water
is exhibited in the form of mists, clouds, dew, or
rain. It has been stated by the late Dr. Hutton
of Edinburgh, and more fully exemplified by Dr.
Dalton, that the quantity of vapour capable of
entering into air, increases in a greater ratio than
the temperature; therefore, whenever two volumes
of air, of different temperatures, are mixed together, (each being previously saturated with vapour,)
the mean temperature is not able to support the
mean quantity of vapour; consequently its precipi-
tation in the form of clouds and rain, is occasioned,
not by mere cold, but by a mixture of comparatively
cold and warm air: and on this principle may be
explained many of the phenomena of mist or fog,
clouds, dew, and rain.

Different portions of the earth's surface, and of
course the contiguous portions of air, are differently
heated by the sun's rays impinging upon them in
various degrees of obliquity; and this difference is
naturally much greater in a mountainous than in a
champaign country; and on two portions of air
thus unequally heated, being intermixed one with
the other—either by the ascent of the warmer and
lighter part, or by a gentle current of the wind—
the vapour assumes a visible form.

The temperature of the earth, from a few yards
below the surface, to the greatest depth hitherto
explored, suffers little variation between summer
and winter. It corresponds nearly with the mean
temperature of the atmosphere; being here about

48 degrees of Fahrenheit's thermometer. A body
of water, such as a lake of considerable depth,
forms a kind of mean between the subjacent earth
and the superincumbent air: its surface is influenced by the temperature of the atmosphere, while
its lower parts admit of less variation; consequently
the surface will in summer be the warmest, and in
winter the coldest part. So long as the surface
of water retains its fluidity, it helps to meliorate
the temperature of the air in its vicinity; and its
surface being frozen, the water contiguous to the
ice will always be nearly 32°; at the same time
the temperature towards the bottom may be some
degrees higher.

In clear weather, the surface both of the earth
and of water is warmed in the day and cooled
during the night; but in different proportions—the
water retaining its heat much longer than the land.
It will sometimes happen, in an autumnal evening,
that the temperature of the air and that of the
water of a lake will be equal; and yet before sun-
rise there will be a difference of twenty degrees
or upwards; in this case the air above the water,
being warmer, will contain more vapour than that
above the land, and on their intermixture a mist
or fog will be formed; which will continue to float
in the atmosphere till it be either dissolved by an
increase of heat, or being moved into a colder
region, be deposited in the form of dew or hoar
frost. Sir Humphrey Davy has observed, that
upon some rivers on the continent, a mist or fog

began to appear as soon as the temperature of the air was diminished from 3 to 6 degrees below that of the water. This will depend upon the previous moisture or dryness of the air, and partly on the current of the wind; but a fog is seldom seen on these lakes, until the difference of temperature reaches 12 degrees or upwards.

On the disappearance of the sun in a clear evening, a mist is sometimes observed over a piece of moist ground; where it seems to be formed, and for some time kept afloat, by a kind of contention between the heated surface of the earth below it, and the colder atmosphere above; but the earth not continuing to afford the necessary supply of heat, the conflict ceases; and the vapour settles upon the grass in the shape of dew.

It has been a matter of surprise to some, that a cloud should seem to remain stationary upon the summit of a high mountain, when the air was moving at a brisk rate. The warm air of a valley being impelled up the inclined plane of a mountain side, into a colder region, is not able to support the same quantity of vapour; and a cloud is formed in consequence; and although the individual particles of which it is composed, are continually moving forward with the wind; yet by a perpetual accession of vapour on one side, and dispersion on the other, the cloud may continue to occupy the same place, and appear to a distant observer as stationary; although its component parts are successively changed: and in this manner may the

Q 2

materials of a cloud be transported invisibly from the summit of one mountain to that of another.

When a dense cloud settles upon a mountain, the wind frequently blows from it on one side with an increased momentum, while on the opposite side its motion is retarded; and a shower commencing on the hills, is generally preceded in its course by a squall—the air, displaced by the falling rain, making its escape along the valleys where it meets with the least resistance.

A covering of snow makes a kind of barrier, between the internal heat of the earth, and that of the atmosphere: being a bad conductor, it preserves the surface of the earth from the severity of cold in winter; but in spring, excludes it from the genial effects of the solar rays. In the meantime the contiguous atmosphere suffers more extensive variations; the greatest extreme of cold being experienced when the earth is covered with snow.

The quantity of rain seems to increase as we approach from the south towards the great group of the Cumbrian mountains; which probably receive more rain than any equal area in England: the annual average being at London little more than 20 inches; at Manchester 36 inches; at Kendal 56; and in the neighbourhood of Windermere and Esthwaite, upwards of 70 inches. On the north of the mountains again, it decreases; at Keswick being estimated at 58, while at Carlisle it does not much exceed 30 inches.

# THE FLOATING ISLAND

## IN DERWENT LAKE.

SOME have contended that the term Floating
Island was improperly applied to this subject, as
it never changes its situation—being still attached
by its sides to the adjacent earth under water;
but Floating Island being the name by which it
has always been known, there can be no manifest
impropriety in retaining the appellation.

It is situated in the south-east corner of the
lake, not far from Lowdore, about 150 yards from
the shore, where the depth of the water does not
exceed six feet in a mean state of the lake. It
generally rises after an interval of a few years,
and after a continuance of warm weather. Its
figure and dimensions are variable: it has sometimes contained about half an acre of ground, at
other times only a few perches; but extending in
a gradual slope under water, a much greater portion is raised from the bottom than reaches the
surface of the lake. Several large rents or cracks
may be seen in the earth about the place, which
appear to have been occasioned by its stretching
to reach the surface. It never rises far above the

level of the lake; but having once attained the
surface, it, for a time, fluctuates with the rise and
fall of the water; after which it sinks gradually.
When at rest in the bottom of the lake, it has the
same appearance as the neighbouring parts, being
covered with the same vegetation, consisting principally of *Littorella lacustris*, and *Lobelia dort-
manna*, interspersed with *Isoetes lacustris*, and
other plants common in this and all the neighbouring lakes: after remaining some time above
the water, its verdure is much improved.   For a
few inches in depth it is composed of a clayey or
earthy matter, apparently deposited by the water,
in which the growing plants have fixed their roots;
the rest is a congeries of decayed vegetable matter,
forming a stratum of loose peat earth about six
feet in thickness; which rises from a bed of very
fine soft clay.   A considerable quantity of air is
contained in the body of the island, and may be
dislodged by probing the earth with a pole.   This
air has been found by Dr. Dalton to consist of
equal parts of carburetted hydrogen and azotic
gasses, with a little carbonic acid.

In the last forty years, the times of its appearance have been as follows.   In 1808, from the
20th July to the beginning of October; in 1813,
from the 7th September to the end of October;
in 1815, from the 5th to the end of August; in
1819, from the 14th August to the end of that
month; in 1824, from 21st June to the end of
September; in 1825, it was above water from the

9th to the 23rd of September; and in 1826, from the 11th July to the end of September; the uncommon circumstance of its appearing in three successive years, may be attributed to the extraordinary warmth of the seasons. It rose above water again on the 10th June, 1831, and remained uncovered till the 24th September, being the longest period ever remembered; although its dimensions have sometimes been larger. In 1834 and 1835 it was above water, for a few weeks in each year, in August and September; and in 1837, in July and August. Again, in 1841, it appeared on the 19th of July, and remained till the beginning of the following month.

It would be tedious to investigate every hypothesis which has from time to time been put forth to account for this phenomenon—with the arguments for and against each—some supposing water, others air, as the chief agent in its production.

A small mountain stream which pours down a rock opposite the place, and runs underground before it reaches the lake, has been employed in various ways to account for its rising; and many an assumption has been advanced, of the way in which air might be conveyed or generated underneath it.

One material circumstance has however generally escaped observation: namely, that the air to which the rising of this island has been attributed, is not collected in a body underneath it; but is interspersed through the whole mass. And the most probable conclusion seems to be, that air or gas is generated in the body of the island by decomposition of the vegetable matter of which it is formed; and this gas being produced most copiously, as well as being more rarefied in hot weather, the earth at length becomes so much distended therewith, as to render the mass of less weight than an equal bulk of water. The water then insinuating itself between the substratum of clay and the peat earth forming the island, bears it to the surface, where it continues for a time; till, partly by escape of the gas, partly by its absorption, and partly by its condensation consequent on a decrease of heat, the volume is reduced; and the earth gradually sinks to its former level, where it remains till a sufficient accumulation of gas again renders it buoyant.

But as the vegetable matter of which the island is principally composed, appears to have been amassed at a remote period, when the lake was of less depth than at present, receiving very little addition from the decay of plants recently grown upon the spot; it is reasonable to suppose that the process furnishing the gas cannot from the same materials be continued *ad infinitum:* but that there must be, or probably may have been, a time when it shall have arrived at its maximum: after which the eruptions will become less extensive or less frequent.

# THE BLACK LEAD MINE

## IN BORROWDALE.

Of the first discovery or opening of this mine, we have no account; but from a conveyance made in the beginning of the seventeenth century, it appears to have been known and estimated before that time. The manor of Borrowdale is said to have belonged to the Abbey of Furness; and having at the dissolution of that monastery fallen to the crown, it was granted by James the First to William Whitmore and Jonas Verdon, who by a deed bearing date the twenty-eighth day of November 1614, sold and conveyed unto Sir Wilfred Lawson and thirty-six others therein named, all the said manor of Borrowdale, "except all those wad-holes and wad, commonly called black cawke, within the commons of Seatollar, or elsewhere within the commons and wastes of the manor of Borrowdale aforesaid, of the yearly rent or value of fifteen shillings and four-pence;" since which time it has been held distinct from other royalties of the manor; a family of the name of Bankes being for some generations the principal proprietors.

It is situated about nine miles from Keswick, in the steep side of a mountain, near the head of

the valley of Borrowdale; and occurs in a rock
called, by Mr. Bakewell, a grey felspar porphry.
It is not found in a continuous vein; but rather in
sops or bellies, the connection between which is
traced with difficulty.

Formerly this mine was worked only at intervals,
and when a sufficient quantity had been procured
to supply the demand for a few years, it was strongly
closed up until the stock was reduced; but of late
it has been obtained less plentifully, and the demand being greater, the working has been continued for several years successively.

Being capable of enduring a great heat without
fusing, or cracking, it is used in the manufacture of
crucibles; it is excellent in diminishing friction in
machinery; and its value in cleaning and glossing
cast-iron work is known to every housemaid.　But
its principal use is in pencils, for the manufacture
of which Keswick has been long famed; but though
in the vicinity of the mine, the pencil-makers are
obliged to purchase all their black-lead in London,
as the proprietors will not permit any to be sold
until it has first been lodged in their own warehouse.　It was formerly used without any previous
preparation; being only cut with a saw to the
scantlings required, and thus enclosed in a suitable casing of cedar wood; but generally being too
soft for some purposes, a method of hardening it
had long been a desideratum; and a process has
at length been discovered, by which it may be
rendered capable of bearing a finer and more

durable point; but its colour will be somewhat deteriorated.

Great quantities of pencils are now made of a composition, formed of the saw-dust and small pieces of black-lead, which being ground to an impalpable powder, is mixed with some cohesive medium: for this purpose different substances are employed, some of which make a very inferior pencil; but others, being united at a proper degree of heat, and consolidated by a strong pressure, make a pencil to answer for many purposes, (especially where the writing is intended to be permanent,) full as well as the genuine black-lead.

The specific gravity of the best wad, or black-lead, is, to that of water, as two to one nearly: the coarser kind is heavier in proportion, as it contains more stony matter. It comes from the mine in pieces of irregular shape, and of various sizes, requiring no process to prepare it for the market, further than freeing the pieces from rock, or any extraneous matter which may adhere to them. It is then assorted according to the different degrees of purity and size, and thus packed in casks and sent off to the warehouse in London, where it is exposed to sale only on the first Monday in every month.

To prevent the depredations of intruders, it has sometimes been necessary to keep a strong guard upon the place; and for its better protection, an Act of Parliament was passed 25th George II. cap. 10th, by which an unlawful entering of any mine, or wad-hole of wad, or black-cawke, commonly called black-lead, or unlawfully taking or carrying away any wad, &c. therefrom, as also the buying or receiving the same, knowing it to be unlawfully taken, is made felony.

In the year 1803, after a tedious search, one of the largest bellies was fallen in with, which produced five hundred casks, weighing about one hundred and a quarter each, and worth thirty shillings a pound and upwards, besides a greater quantity of inferior sorts; and since that time several smaller sops have been met with: in the beginning of the year 1829, a sop produced about half a dozen casks; the best part of which was eagerly bought up at thirty-five shillings a pound. In 1833, they succeeded in filling a few casks, the best part of which has been sold at forty-five shillings a pound; since which time it has been less productive.

The annual consumption of this mineral, which two hundred years ago had been valued at fifteen shillings and four-pence, has been estimated at between 3,000*l.* and 4,000*l.*, and appears to be constantly increasing; but how far a permanency of supply can be calculated upon, is questionable. The most prolific part of the mountain may be already explored, and the principal body or trunk of the mine excavated, so that posterity must be contented with gleaning from the branches.

LANCASTER.

# LONSDALE, AND THE CAVES.

In enumerating the various paths by which the Lake District may be approached, mention has been made in this volume (p. 91) of the line from Lancaster up the vale of Lune, through Kirkby Lonsdale, to Kendal. It has been suggested that the first portion of this route is of sufficient importance to justify a more lengthened description; and that a few pages may be well devoted to an account of the Caves and other natural curiosities, which may be conveniently visited from Kirkby Lonsdale.

The details which follow, are presented to the tourist by one who is personally acquainted with the scenes he describes; but who, in matters veiled in the obscurity of ancient days, is content to rely upon the opinions of antiquarians of repute, (such as Dr. Whittaker,) whose decisions are more deserving of regard than any hypothesis which he might presume to propound.

LANCASTER.—Dr. Whittaker pronounces Lancaster "a highly favoured place, distinguished by the beauty of its situation, the magnificence of its castle, and its rank as the capital of one of the most populous counties in the kingdom." The complaisance of antiquaries, led by their father, Camden, has generally induced them to consider this place as the *Longoricus* of the *Notitiæ*; but Dr. W. conceives it to have been the *Setantiorum Portus* of Ptolemy. At this time, "an attentive eye will scarcely discover, in the oldest remaining buildings, any vestiges of architecture prior to the time of Charles II."—*The Castle* well deserves the inspection of the visitor, to whom the interior is accessible at all hours of the day. The Gateway, flanked by two octagonal turrets, surmounted by watch towers, and defended by a triple row of machicolations, is appropriated to John of Gaunt, by the arms of himself and his royal father. It is about 66 feet in height. The new buildings, including the two splendid Courts, were commenced in 1788, and completed at an expense to the county of £40,000.——*The Church*. This is an edifice chiefly erected in the 12th century. It is 143 feet in length, 58 feet in breadth, and 40 feet in height; situated closely adjacent to the Castle, in a spacious Church-yard, from whence the most beautiful views are obtained.  The most valuable relics, the Stalls, have, according to Whittaker, been probably brought hither from some more stately building.——*The Town Hall,* an imposing structure in the Market-place, was built in 1781–3, at an expense of £1,300.——*The Lunatic Asylum,* a building admirably adapted for the melancholy purpose for which it was erected, may be viewed by tickets granted by the Visiting Justices.  It is situated on the Moor, a mile east of the Town.

## THE VALLEY

There are two routes from Lancaster to Kirkby Lonsdale; one by Halton, on the western, the other by Hornby, on the eastern side of the river. The former is shorter by two miles, but, being hilly and uninteresting, the latter route is generally preferred—as it ought to be by all who wish to see the country.  " On approaching Caton, three miles from Lancaster," says Dr. Whittaker, " the character of the Vale of Lune, as one of the first of northern valleys, is instantly and incontrovertibly established.  The noble windings of the river, the fruitful alluvial lands on its banks, the woody and cultivated ridge which bounds it to the north-west, the striking feature of Hornby Castle in front, and, above all, the noble form of Ingleborough, certainly compose an assemblage not united in any rival scenery in the kingdom."  Before reaching Caton, on the

high ground, a little to the right of the road, is
the view up the valley, described and rendered
celebrated by the poet Gray.

"At Hornby, a fine opening to the right, consisting of the valleys formed by the Wenning and
the Greta, discloses new scenes of beauties, again
terminated by Ingleborough, now seen in nearer
and more distinct majesty; after which, the principal opening, growing still more expanded, and
suffering nothing, as yet, from its increased elevation, either in point of shade or fertility, approaches
Kirkby Lonsdale. The soft and luxuriant beauties
of this place, terminated by the Howgill Fells, a
group of mountains, of striking form, though inferior to Ingleborough, are scarcely to be surpassed:
and he who should wish for a happier combination
of river, meadows, and indigenous wood of the
richest growth, than that which appears beneath
the celebrated terrace of this place, might have
cause to lament that his taste was too fastidious to
admit of any gratification from landscape. As we
advance northward, the vale gradually undergoes
some diminution of its charms, though none of its
fertility, till it is met by the Rothay, from the
east. It then assumes, more and more, the character of a high mountain glen, gradually ascending and contracting, while it grows diminutive in
its features, as well as cold and barren in proportion, till, after a rapid turn towards the east, the
glen and brook of Lune terminate on the verge of
Ravenstonedale, in Westmorland."

CLAUGHTON—"the Town of Claugh"—possesses an ancient Manor House, built about the latter end of James, or the beginning of Charles I. It is of an oblong form, with two embattled towers, containing numerous transome lights.

HORNBY, — "unquestionably the Manse of Horne, a Saxon name,"—is a neat little town, watered by the river Wenning, and situated at the confluence of that river with the Lune. The site of the *Castle* was anciently occupied by the Romans. The first structure, of which there are no remains, is attributed by Camden to Nicholas de Montbegon, who flourished about the 12th century, or 1st of Henry I. The Great Tower was built by Edward, the first Lord Mounteagle, whose name and motto may be seen upon it. The Eagle Tower, which surmounts it, was erected by Lord Wemyss, in 1743; and the present Front by the Chartres family. Independently of other associations connected with this place, it will long be remembered as the subject of "The Great Will Cause," which, commenced in 1826, is only just brought to a conclusion—a striking instance of "the law's delay."

The *Church* was begun by Edward, Lord Mounteagle, in consequence, as tradition reports, of a vow made on Flodden Field. The octagon tower alone, which retains his arms, encircled with the Garter, was finished by himself. It bears the following inscription:

E. Stanley: miles: dux: Mounteagle: me: fieri: fecit.

The choir was completed by his executors in an inferior manner. In the Churchyard remains the tall base of a very singular and ancient cross, (a ponderous block of free-stone.)

To the west of the Church is a small Catholic Chapel, the officiating priest of which is Dr. Lingard, the celebrated historian, who lives in the residence adjoining.

ANCIENT MOUNDS.—The traveller through Lunesdale cannot but be struck with numerous artificial mounds, which greet his eye in every direction. About half a mile from Hornby, on the road to Gressingham, is the most remarkable of these ancient works. According to Dr. Whittaker, "this is a magnificent Saxon fortification, intended to guard the pass of the Lune, as it commands the river upwards and downwards. Its form is a regular ellipsis, at the north end of which the axis major is a circular mount, separated from the area below by an interior second fosse. The whole area is 2A. 9P. It is, perhaps, not too bold a conjecture, to suppose that it was the Castle of Horne, the first founder." It has been assumed by other writers that these elevations constitute the *Agraria* of the Romans. It is remarkable that a majority of them are situated near our old parish churches: for instance, at Halton, Melling, Arkholme, Kirkby Lonsdale, and Sedbergh. For whatever purpose they were originally designed, whether as places of defence, or "moot-hills," where justice was dispensed; in later days, they appear to have been

put to more ignoble uses. " I find," says Whittaker, "'The Gallow Hill of Melling' mentioned in
the records of Hornby Castle." And the small
one, on the glebe immediately behind the Vicarage
at Kirkby Lonsdale, appears to have been used for
even a less useful and more cruel purpose, being
known to this day by the *soubriquet* of " Cock-pit
Hill."

MELLING. Proceeding up the valley, two miles
from Hornby, we pass through Melling. The
Church a spacious building of late Gothic, is remarkable for nothing but a rich Norman doorway,
and a handsome black-marble font presented by
W. Gillison Bell, Esq., whose residence is the
Hall contiguous, which commands an extensive and
diversified view upwards of the expanded vale.

THURLAND CASTLE.

Crossing the Greta, we approach THURLAND
CASTLE, in a spacious park. It was built in the
reign of Henry IV. and left in ruins by the rava-
ges of the wars of Charles I. It has however been
judiciously restored by R. T. North, Esq. the present proprietor; in the process of which the demo-
lition of the hoary gateway is to be lamented.

Brian Tunstall, "the stainless," "that bold 'squire," who fell on Flodden Field, held Thurland Castle and the lordship; and is said to lie buried in Tunstall Church; but Whittaker doubts the latter fact, and assigns the recumbent statue which now lies near the altar rails, and which tradition points out as his effigy, "with little diffidence" to Sir Thomas Tunstall, the founder of the Castle.

On the right, a quarter of a mile from the village of Tunstall, stands the Church, a plain fabric of middle Gothic.

A mile onward is OVERBOROUGH, or Burrow. The stranger cannot but be delighted with the appearance which this place presents—its cottages overgrown with roses and woodbines; and the small garden plots in front, blooming with fragrant flowers, and verdant with laurels and rhododendrons.

ROMAN STATION.——Immediately on passing Leck Beck, we arrive on "classic ground,"—the site of the *Bremetonacæ* of Antonine. Burrow Hall, a respectable mansion of the last century, is erected upon the Prætorium.

A drive of two miles brings us to KIRKBY LONS-DALE BRIDGE. The date of this noble structure is lost in obscurity. There is no doubt, however, that it was built previous to the time of Edward the First; as it appears that in the third year of that reign, a rate of pontage was granted for repairs. It is built of freestone, and has three ribbed arches, the two larger of the span of 55 feet each, and the smallest of 28 feet. The roadway is 180 feet in length, but so narrow that "two wheelbarrows tremble when they meet." The views of the river from the centre are singularly beautiful; it here flows through a rocky channel, narrow, but of profound depth; and the banks on either side are adorned with fine trees. In the spring of 1841, a drover committed suicide by precipitating himself over the parapet on the north side into the water —a height of 45 feet.

KIRKBY LONSDALE contains upwards of 1200 inhabitants. It is the capital of, says Dr. Whittaker, "probably the finest valley in the kingdom," and was formerly, as its name implies, the Kirk or Church Town of Lunesdale. It possesses a too spacious market-place. The only building of any importance is the Church. The architectural effect of this venerable edifice has been entirely destroyed. We are indebted to the execrable taste of some modern Goths for its present barn-like appearance; its leaden roofs, battlements, pinnacles, and clear story, having been removed to give place to an enormous sweeping roof of blue slate. In the

interior, it is as bad. The same rage for improvement has pulled down stalls and carved work; and covered, with a thick coat of plaster, column and capital of the most delicate and elaborate workmanship.    The western doorway is a rich Norman

arch, adorned with basso relievos of grotesque animals, &c.    After leaving the church, proceed through the stile in the north-east corner of the church-yard, and take a survey of the view alluded to at p. 186. Pursuing the path along the

Brow, and through a fine park, you shortly come in sight of Underley, erected by A. Nowell, Esq., but now the property of Alderman Thompson, M. P.

From Kirkby Lonsdale, the tourist to the Lakes may proceed direct to Kendal, but, if his time permit, a drive up the valley will be found replete with interest.

CASTERTON HALL.

A mile from Kirkby Lonsdale, on the eastern side of Lune, is CASTERTON, the Pride of Lons-

S

dale. Two or three hours spent amongst its woods, hermitages, gardens, cascades, and fountains, will yield an ample store of enjoyment; and a visit to its admirable scholastic institutions, established by The Rev. W. Carus Wilson, will afford to the philanthropist a gratification of no ordinary kind.

Four miles further, on the left, is Grimeshill, the residence of Wm. Moore, Esq., the representative of an ancient Westmorland family; and half a mile further, on the right, is Middleton Hall, an excellent specimen of our ancient manor houses.

Cross the Rothay, and proceed up the valley, in a westerly direction, to the Black Horse in Killington, or more commonly " Scotch Jean's." From the hill immediately in front of the house, there is a very splendid view of the vales of Lune, Rothay, and Garsdale.

Onwards, about six miles further we come to Low Borrow Bridge. It is situated in the northern pass of the valley, at its junction with Little Borrodale. There is an excellent inn here, where parties may form head quarters, while visiting the vicinity. Here is a Roman Station, now called Castle Field, close behind the house; consisting of a square inclosure, 360 feet in length, and 300 in breadth. On the sides facing the east, north, and west, are the remains of the walls; and on the latter side, the traces of two fosses. Where the east gate stood, is a stone, which was dug out a few years ago, and it is evidently one of the original sockets, the groove for the hinge remaining as perfect as if freshly cut. Sherds of Roman pottery have been found; and a silver coin of the reign of Aurelian. From the style of the cutting or quartering of the facing stones, (many of which have been used in building the outhouses, in order to preserve them,) there is no doubt that this station is coeval with Overborough, and is the site of the long lost and much disputed *Alone*. The very name seems to warrant this opinion; for it is the first station on the Lune (or Lone); and what so natural as to give it the title from the river which watered its walls? The remains of several buildings have been discovered between the eastern wall and the river.

From Borrow Bridge, The Black Force and Cautley Spout may be conveniently visited; but only by pedestrians.

THE BLACK FORCE is a place frequented by few but the shepherds, and should not be attempted without a guide. It is a most terrific scene when visited in an evening. An enormous hollow in the mountain, about a quarter of a mile in length, and of an immense depth, yawns before you. You enter, and find a chasm, whose black walls seem to reach the top of the hill; at the upper end of which is a cascade, whose stream is lost in spray before it reaches the bottom, which is strewed with enormous fragments of rock. Cross the eastern side of the ravine, and, still keeping the water side, proceed for another quarter of a mile, when you can ascend the mountain, which was before impracticable. When you arrive at the summit, look

at the views around you, which are well worth all
the labour you have undergone.   From the top of
this mountain (Fell Heud) it is an easy journey to

CAUTLEY SPOUT.   This place, though not properly belonging to Lonsdale, is too important a
feature of the Howgill Fells to be omitted.   It
consists of three cascades; the highest of which
takes a clear leap of 400 feet and upwards.   The
whole height of the cascade, from the "spout" to
the foot of the lower fall, has been measured as
860 feet.   The south side of the fall is crowned by
tremendous precipices and shelves of loose stones,
called "Cautley Screes."   The north side is particularly abrupt, and requires a firm foot, and a
good head, to get either up or down.

The tourist is now supposed to have returned
from his trip up the valley, to Kirkby Lonsdale; before he leaves it for the Caves, let him take a view
of the Bridge, from the banks of the river.   The
above is an accurate engraving of it from the north.

## THE CAVES.

ALL the caves may be visited in progression from Kirkby Lonsdale.   To see Yordas, it is necessary to send word to the Guide, who keeps the key of the cavern, which is locked up to prevent the destruction of the petrifactions.   Mr. Whittingdale, of Gale Green, Masongill, performs the office of *cicerone* to Yordas.

We now take the caves in rotation, beginning with Easgill, and ending with Goredale.

SCENE IN EASGILL.

EASGILL is a tremendous rocky ravine betwixt Leck and Casterton fells, abounding in natural

s 2

curiosities.    It is three miles from Kirkby Lonsdale, and may be approached by two routes:—one,
direct, over Low Casterton Fell End; the other
by Cowen Bridge, Leck, and Leck Fell: the latter,
however, is the best carriage route.    Easgill is dry
in the summer months; unless during a thunder
shower, or continued rains.    In the winter season, when the snow is melting, or the clouds
pour down their waters, it is a mountain torrent
of the most rapid and tumultuous nature, forming
a succession of whirlpools, waterfalls, and eddies,
unequalled in Britain.

There is a cavern called the WITCH HOLES,
about 300 yards from the entrance to the gill.    It
is easy of access, and continues for a long way
into the mountain; but, after proceeding about 80
yards, we are stopped by a pool of water.    To
the right of the entrance there is a singular thin
plate of limestone, called the "Witches' staircase;"
on climbing which, you find yourself in a small
apartment, all glittering with innumerable crystals.
The path from the cave to Easgill Kirk is dangerous and difficult.    Pass the "Dangerous Gate,"
on the left side of the gill, over a narrow ledge in
the face of the precipice, and you are at once in

EASGILL KIRK.—You are now standing upon
the primitive pavement of a river's bed, forming
an area of at least 200 yards in circumference,
inclosed on all sides but one by gigantic perpendicular cliffs, rising from one to two hundred feet,
and ornamented at the top, and in various parts of

the sides, by trees, shrubs, and creeping plants. In time of floods, there is a beautiful fall of water in the north-east corner, of about 30 feet; and another in the "Choir," a little to the right. The Choir is entered by a fine arch, 8 feet high, and 14 feet broad. The interior is a small lofty apartment; and just over the entrance, on the opposite side, is a grotesque petrifaction suspended from the roof, called "The Priest of Easgill."

Climb the hill on the south-west side of the Kirk, and take a narrow path which winds along the summit, from which there is a fine view into the interior. Descend again into the bed of the river above, and you have, on either side, particularly on the south, a range of high cliffs, having the appearance of a large fort in ruins. About a quarter of a mile up the ravine, you come in sight of

The Force. It is of smaller dimensions than the Kirk, and of a different character. On standing at the entrance, it reminded us of nothing so strongly as the stage of a theatre prepared for a Brigand scene. Thin pieces of rock project from the sides, nearly into the middle of the area, and a large oblong loophole, of singular construction, admits the water at the furthest, or eastern extremity. The rocks rise to a considerable height on each side, and are, as usual, fringed with trees, which almost overshadow it.

These fells abound with chasms of profound depth, and several small caves, which are difficult of access. The most remarkable are Bull-pot, Gavel-pot, and Rumbling Hole.

ENTRANCE TO YORDAS.

YORDAS CAVE.—The nearest route from Easgill to Yordas, is to proceed in a south-easterly
direction to the top of Gregareth, the lofty mountain to the right of the Force.   On arriving at the
summit, descend again in the same line, taking
care to look out for a small plantation on your side
of the road through Kingsdale, which is in sight.
This plantation clothes the rocky banks of a small
ravine, down which flows a stream of water, in a
succession of small cascades, until it suddenly
rushes out of sight, being swallowed by a large
fissure in the rock.   At the foot of the ravine, is
the entrance into Yordas Cave, forming a regular
arch about 7 feet high, and 8 feet wide.   On gain-
ing admittance, the guide fixes an ample number
of candles upon two cross pieces of wood at the end
of a long pole; the visitor, also, takes one in each
hand.   You then proceed under a low rock, which

hangs to within 5 feet of the floor. After proceeding a few yards, the cave seems interminable, as
the eye is not quite accustomed to the gloom; and
the rushing of a large body of water, reverberating
through the hollow space, causes a feeling of awe.
A brook runs through the entire length of the
cave, which has been called the "River Styx."
You are now in a magnificent hall, 180 feet long,
48 feet in breadth, and from 35 to 70 feet high;
the sides being covered with curious petrifactions.   On the east, they are numerous, and give
one the idea of escutcheons, armour, and trophies,
hung against the wall of some baron's hall.   These
are called "The Brown Bear," "The Coat of
Mail," "The Gauntlet,"
"The Ram's Head,"
and "The Organ;"—
and the likeness to these
different objects is very
striking.  The next place
is the "Bishop's Throne,"
in the north-east corner.
The petrifactions, al-
though of a dusky hue,
are remarkably fine, con-
sisting of wreathed pil-
lars, supporting a canopy.  A little to the left,
through a narrow passage, you arrive at the
" Chapter House." This is the most beautiful
portion of the cavern; being a circular apartment,
the dome of which is supported by slender twisted

columns; the most delicate stalactites hang pendent
from the sides; and at the north end, a fine cascade
falls down a smooth rock, from an elevation of at
least 50 feet.

YORDAS—LOOKING BACK.

From Yordas the tourist may visit Gingling
Cave, Rowton Hole, the Keld Head, Ravenwray,
and Thornton Force; and so on to Ingleton, where
there are good inns.    But if he wishes to proceed
immediately to Weathercote Cove in Chapel-le-
dale, he must cross Kingsdale above Bredagarth,
and ascend the mountain by a rough road, or
track, keeping on the south-west side of a quag-
mire near a heap of stones, apparently a cairn,
on the base of Whernside; and then turning round
the west corner of the mountain, he will find himself near two or three lanes, any of which will lead
him to the chapel in the valley between Whernside
and Ingleborough.    But this route is practicable
only for pedestrians: carriages must go by Thornton Church Stile, and turn there to the left to Yordas, returning by the same road, and thence to Ingleton, whence to Weathercote it is four miles.

Situate in a romantic glen, about a mile from Thornton Church Stile, is THORNTON FORCE, a remarkably fine waterfall. The river here falls, with a noise like thunder, at one leap, about 30 yards, through an opening between two rocks. We stand at the top, surveying the scene, which is extremely wild and picturesque. The rocks are fringed with trees, which impart a certain air of gloom and veneration around the spot; and the spray arising from the deep basin beneath, resembles mist, or wreaths of smoke from a furnace, and sprinkles the ground for many yards around the fall. From below, a picture is exhibited which leaves little for the imagination to supply. The white sheet of flowing water—the black receptacle beneath—the tree-clad rocks—and the wild mountain scenery around, form a landscape as complete as the most fastidious *artiste* could desire.

About 200 yards above the Force, is the rugged pass of RAVENWRAY. Its wild and lofty scenery may be better understood, after perusing the following sonnet:

> Dark frowns the cliff upon the mountain stream,
> That 'cainst its time-worn fragments breaks below,
> And all in unison its waters flow
> With the wild scene around  The wailing scream
> Of the lone raven, from the stunted yew
> Heard ominous—alone its solitude
> Disturbs, and on the awe-struck soul intrude
> Thoughts that its inmost energies subdue
> To their strong working  On the rocks steep
> Dimly the grey-haired Son of Song appears,
> While o'er the harp his airy fingers sweep,
> And at his bidding, forms of other years
> Start into being  mighty men of yore
> Like the wild dream that fashioned them——no more'

D.

The cliff on the west side is a rocky promontory about 40 yards high, spotted with ivy and evergreen shrubs; whilst the Doe runs beneath over fragments of rocks, forming very romantic cascades.

WEATHERCOTE CAVE.—This surprising natural curiosity is of a lozenge form; and its whole length, from north to south, is about 60 yards. It is divided into two parts by a rugged arch of limestone. The entrance is by a door in the southeast side, and you proceed down a flight of rude  steps, under the arch, into the great cave. Here you are full in view of the cascade, which rushes out of a hole in the north corner of the gloomy cavity. Rocks, covered with black moss, rise to the height of 120 feet; and the trees, meeting nearly over the top, add to the gloom and horror of the place. The cascade, however, absorbs all the attention. The exact height of the north corner of the cave is 40 yards, and the aperture whence the water issues is 11 yards from the top, the fall making a clear leap of 29 yards, or 87 feet, upon a large flat rock at the bottom, with a deafening noise, and a concussion which makes the earth seem to tremble.  Between the spectator and the cascade is a fragment of rock, suspended by its opposite angles touching the sides of the crevice.  When the sun shines, a small, but vivid rainbow is formed in the thick spray, which continues about two hours at mid-day.  Af-

ter heavy rains the water pours into this cave on all sides.  All around, thousands of streamlets, some as small as the running of a tap, others copious as a mill-race, hurl themselves into the boiling cavity, which, unable to carry off the deluge, is sometimes full, and flows over its bounds.

GINGLE POT is a natural chasm in the bed of the rock, about 23 yards long, 3 yards broad, and 16 yards deep, 200 yards south of Weathercote. At its southern extremity is a passage leading to the stream, which loses itself in that cave.  When a stone is cast down, it produces a peculiarly hollow and gingling sound, from which, as in the case of Gingling Cave in Gregareth, it derives its name.  During floods, the water boils out of this hole.  It is situated at the foot of a precipice, and is hidden from view by trees.

HURTLE POT is a dismal, gloomy hole, surrounded on all sides with perpendicular rocks,

T

which overhang a deep dark pool of water. The descent to the edge of this pool is by a steep and slippery path; and whenever you speak, or throw in a pebble, your ears are assailed by uncommon noises, whilst your nostrils are affected by unpleasant odours from the ramps and other weeds that grow plentifully about its sides, and the rank vapours that exhale from the black abyss beneath. The depth of the pool, by accurate measurement, is 27 feet. A curious phenomenon occurs in this cavern, caused by the glutting of the water against the surface of rocks, after heavy rains. A singular noise is heard to proceed from the surface of the water, which the country folks call "The Hurtlepot Boggart," or the "Fairy Churn."

THE CHAPEL-I'-TH'-DALE is 80 yards below Hurtlepot. This church in the wilderness is a very humble structure, and its situation is so beautifully described by the erudite author of "The Doctor," that we cannot help quoting him :—" A hermit who could wish his grave to be as quiet as his cell, could find no better resting-place. On three sides there was an irregular low stone wall, rather to mark the limits of the sacred ground, than to enclose it; on the fourth it was bounded by a brook, whose waters proceed by a subterranean channel from Weathercote Cave. Two or three alders and rowan trees hung over the brook, and shed their leaves and seeds into the stream. Some bushy hazels grew at intervals along the lines of the walls, and a few ash trees as the wind had sown

them.   To the east and west some fields adjoined
it, in that state of half cultivation which gives a
human character to solitude; to the south, on the
other side the brook, the common, with its limestone rocks peering everywhere above ground, extended to the foot of Ingleborough.   A craggy
hill, feathered with birch, sheltered it from the
north.   The turf was as soft and fine as that of
the adjoining hills; it was seldom broken, so scanty
was the population to which it was appropriated;
scarcely a thistle or a nettle deformed it, and a few
tomb-stones which had been placed there, were
now themselves half buried.   The sheep came over
the wall when they listed, and sometimes took
shelter in the porch from the storm.   Their voices,
and the cry of the kite wheeling above, were the
only sounds which were heard there, except when
the single bell, which hung in its niche over the
entrance, tinkled for service on the Sabbath-day,
or, with a slower tongue, gave notice that one of
the children of the soil was returning to the earth
from whence he sprung."

GATEKIRK CAVE.—This beautiful cavern is
about a mile and a half north of Weathercote.   It
has two entrances, one north and another south.
There is another passage from the south west, which
has been likened to an orchestra.   The main branch
of the Greet runs through this cave.   The stalactites
and stalagmites are in the greatest profusion and
perfection.   The whole surface of the roof is hung
with grotesque shapes in stone; and the ledge on

the western side is like an image maker's shop, so full is it of stalagmites of every variety of form. There are several alleys branching off the main passage. The water issues from the cavern in a deep, clear, and strong stream, and is broken into a succession of cascades and eddies, shaded by weeping willows and mountain ash, until it loses itself amongst a group of rocks.

Douk Cave is similar to Weathercote, but not heightened by anything so vast or sublime. It is longer and wider, but not so deep; and it lacks the grand feature of the latter, the waterfall, though there is a small cascade issuing from the cavern. To get into this cavern, it is necessary to climb up the face of the cascade; and you find yourself in a long narrow passage with a lofty roof.

Catknot Hole is a small cavern about three miles and a half from Weathercote, and half a mile from Gearstones. It is situated at the foot of the Great Colm or Cam. The river Ribble runs past the mouth of this cave; and its romantic cascades and precipices are worthy of observation.

Alum Pot lies half-a-mile south west of the village of Selside. It is a most awful looking abyss, at least 50 yards in circumference, and has been measured to the depth of 165 feet, or 55 yards, 43 feet of which were in water, and that, too, in a very dry season.

Long Churn is a little farther up the mountain to the right of Alum Pot. All the beautiful stalactites with which this cavern so much abounded, have been removed by cart loads to build artificial grottos.

DICKEN POT is a long passage running in a contrary direction to Long Churn, and it terminates in a lofty dome, called "St. Paul's."

INGLEBOROUGH.—This noble mountain is a prominent feature in the scenery of this portion of the country. From every part, its table land is seen cleaving the skies; and an ascent upon its summit, on a clear day, is one of the most delightful excursions that can be undertaken. It stands upon a base of at least thirty miles in circumference, and its highest elevation is 2361 feet above the level of the sea. The views from the top are splendid. The whole extent of country from the north to the south, with the Irish sea in the west, can be distinctly traced as in a map. In the north-west, the confused heaps of mountains in the Lake district, with their grotesque outlines, terminate the prospect, at a distance of 50 miles. Westwards, it is closed in by the blending of sea and sky. Southwards, after following the indented shores of the Irish Sea, the Welsh mountains lift their broken summits across the horizon. In the east and north-east, black and irregular hills, and deeply-indented valleys, soon terminate the prospect. The plain on the top is about a mile round; and near the western edge a tower is erected on the spot formerly occupied by a fire-beacon. Several springs rise near the summit, which generally lose themselves in deep chasms in the sides, the most remarkable of which is Mier Gill. There are a number of cavities all over the mountain, resembling inverted cones; the most remarkable is " Barefoot Wives' Hole," a large funnel-shaped pit, 50 yards in diameter, and about 26 yards deep. It is always dry, the water which may flow into it being swallowed amongst the loose stones at the bottom. These pits are similar to those found on the Mounts Etna and Vesuvius. Ingleborough, or " The Station of Fire," has doubtless been, in the time of the Romans, a place of defence, and a beacon of " smoke by day and fire by night" to communicate the intelligence of any irruption or insurrection to the surrounding castelli and encampments.

CLAPHAM is a sweet village, about four miles south of Ingleton, on the Settle road. About a mile and a half from hence is a cavern, which, for magnitude and beauty, is second to none in the British dominions. It may be visited on application to Mr. J. Harrison, the guide, who resides near the church. The walk to it is delightful, the road leading through the pleasure-grounds of Ingleborough, the residence of J. W. Farrer, Esq., Master in Chancery. The path lies for a short distance on the margin of a small artificial lake, and then, turning to the left, enters a deep valley, surrounded by lofty, precipitous hills, abounding in tremendous scars.

At length you arrive at " INGLEBOROUGH CAVE." The entrance is at the base of an immense precipice of limestone, and forms a wide low arch, which gradually narrows for about six yards, where there is an iron grating and a gate, kept constantly locked, save for the ingress and egress of visitors. To describe the interior of this cave is impossible—no language can convey an idea of its beauties—and the journey through it is so free from danger that little children may go to the end of it with impunity. For the first 200 yards, the roof gradually lowers, from about fifteen to five feet. The surface is groined and crossed like elaborate gothic work, but the petrifactions are mostly of a dusky hue, though of every variety of form and size. This portion is called the "Old Cave." It was only in 1837 or 1838 that access was gained into the "New Cave," by letting off the water. Now, however, it is a stupendous cavern, said to be 1000 yards in length, forming a succession of chambers, lobbies, &c., adorned with stalactites and stalagmites of infinite variety, single and grouped. A small stream of water flows through it, which tends to keep the air in agitation, and a path has been raised the whole way, so that visitors may walk through perfectly dry. The utmost care is very properly taken to prevent visitors from injuring the petrifactions, which have been and are forming the most beautiful natural curiosity that can possibly be conceived. A little farther up the glen is "Crow Gill," a crevice in the mountain, similar to Easgill Kirk.

SETTLE may be approached by two routes, both

of which are equally interesting. The first is by the common road, including Buckhaw Brow, and the ebbing and flowing well. The other, turning off at Cross Streets, leads the tourist through the retired hamlet of Lawkland, with its fine old hall, built in the reign of Elizabeth, and having been in the possession of the Inglebys from that period. The present resident is Thomas Ingleby, Esq. By this latter route, the road lies through the town of Giggleswick, in the church-yard of which is the burial-place of Archdeacon Paley. Half a mile from Giggleswick is Settle, a flourishing town —the mart of the Craven district. A handsome Town Hall has lately been erected here, which contains an extensive library, and an excellent news-room. The most remarkable feature of the place is an enormous rock, called Castleber, which raises its *brusque* front over the eastern portion of the town, and seems to threaten it with destruction. At its base are various shady serpentine walks, and seats; and the summit is easily ascended by a pathway cut in the rock. Here a succession of very beautiful views is obtained of the valley of the Ribble, with Pennygant in the north, and Pendlehill in the south; while, to the northwest, the top of Ingleborough is just seen rising behind the rugged summit of the hill above Mains Park.

Proceeding northwards, on the western side of the Ribble, through the palace-village of Stackhouse, the tourist will be highly pleased with the romantic scenery of the valley. After travelling within about a quarter of a mile from Little Stainforth, we come to an old doorway in the wall on the right side of the road, and passing through that, and over a stile in another wall which runs off at right angles, and then turning to the left for about fifty yards, there are a few scattered stones lying around a sort of natural drain. This is called "Robin Hood's Mill;" and if the ear is put to the aperture, as closely as possible, a sound as of rumbling machinery is distinctly heard.

From hence, proceed through Little Stainforth to STAINFORTH FORCE, which lies about fifty yards south of the bridge over the Ribble. This pretty cascade is formed by a succession of steppes or ledges in the strata which form the bed of the river, until it ends in a fall of six or seven feet.

Proceed to Stainforth, and inquire the road to CATTERICK FORCE, a splendid waterfall, about half-a mile from the village. This spot is similar in detail to Easgill, but having a perpetual supply of water, its effect is always sublime.

We are now on our nearest route to Malham and Goredale. The road lies over the tops of the mountains for about six miles, when we come to Malham Tarn, a fine mountain lake, well stored with trout of considerable size and delicate flavour. Two miles farther brought us to

MALHAM COVE, one of the most tremendous precipices which can be conceived. It stretches across the whole width of the valley, forming a natural barricade of stone of every variety of shade, nearly 300 feet high. A stream of water—

the source of the Aire—flows from a small cavity at its base. When viewed from a distance, it has the appearance of an immense ruin, being apparently pierced with ornamental windows and doorways. Half a mile from the Cove is the village of Malham, and another mile brings us to

GOREDALE. In writing of this stupendous and magnificent work of Nature, to which nothing in Britain is comparable, language must fail to de-

scribe, and imagination cease to conceive. To
direct the curious traveller into the gorge, and
there leave him to his own sensations, is all we
can do. The approach is through a rocky ravine,
(strewn with immense fragments, and intersected
by one or two small streams) which gradually narrows and grows more gloomy as we progress.
The rocks on each side rise to an enormous height,
and are the habitations of kites and ravens. At
length, on turning round an awful looking precipitous shoulder of rock, the horrors of the dismal
gorge, and the almost closing precipices burst upon
the sight; whilst the din of the foaming waters,
and the rushing of the winds through the narrow
crevice, heighten the terror of the scene, which is
still further enhanced
by a cliff 240 feet high,
which threatens every
moment to hurl de-
struction on the heads
of those who stand un-
derneath its seeming-
ever-falling bulk. An
adventurous person
may climb above the
lower fall to another,
which rushes from a
round aperture in the
cliffs above. The whole may also be surveyed
from the top.

Leaving Goredale, we follow the course of the

stream for about half a mile, when we are shewn a very pretty cascade, which falls a height of about 30 feet, close by a natural cavity in the rock, called "Janet's Cave." We then visit the River Head, a series of powerful springs, and at length arrive at Kirkby Malham, where there is a fine old church.

The preceding are the chief curiosities in the Districts of Lonsdale and Ewcross: although the tourist may and will find many others of less note, perhaps as beautiful. Our object, however, has been merely to direct him to the leading features of the landscape, leaving him to find out the rest by his own tact and taste. Having derived much pleasure and profit from our visits to these scenes, we should wish all men to participate with us the feelings which spring from a review of the beauties and wonders of Creation.     𝔚. 𝔚. 𝔇.

Kirkby Lonsdale, July, 1842.

KIRKBY LONSDALE BRIDGE.—SOUTH VIEW.

# INDEX.

U

## LIST OF THE ILLUSTRATIONS.

Most of the following Illustrations are from accurate drawings by Mr. T Binns, Portrait Painter, Halifax, and they are all engraven by Mr. O. Jewitt, of Headington, Oxford

ARTHUR FOSTER, PRINTER, KIRKBY LONSDALE.

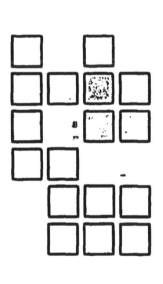

# Through the Devil's Eye

The Air Cadets

C.R. Cummings

## *Also By*
# CHRISTOPHER CUMMINGS

*The Green Idol of Kanaka Creek*

*Ross River Fever*

*Train to Kuranda*

*The Mudskipper Cup*

*Davey Jones's Locker*

*Below Bartle Frere*

*Airship Over Atherton*

*Cockatoo*

*The Cadet Corporal*

*Stannary Hills*

*Coast of Cape York*

*Kylie and the Kelly Gang*

*Behind Mt. Baldy*

*The Cadet Sergeant Major*

*Cooktown Christmas*

*Secret in the Clouds*

*The Word of God*

*The Cadet Under-Officer*

*\*Through the Devil's Eye*

*Barbara and the Smiley People*

# Through the Devil's Eye

The Air Cadets

C.R. Cummings

DoctorZed
Publishing
www.doctorzed.com

Published 2017 by DoctorZed Publishing

DoctorZed Publishing books may be ordered through booksellers or by contacting:

DoctorZed Publishing
10 Vista Ave
Skye, South Australia 5072
www.doctorzed.com
61-(0)8 8431-4965

ISBN: 978-0-9945542-9-1 (sc)
ISBN: 978-0-6480079-1-3 (e)

National Library of Australia Cataloguing-in-Publication entry

Author: Cummings, C. R., author.
Title: Through the devil's eye / Christopher Cummings.
ISBN: 9780994554291 (paperback)
Series: Cummings, C. R. The air cadets.
Target Audience: For young adults.
Subjects: Adventure stories, Australian.
Military cadets--Queensland--Fiction.

Cover image © Scott Zarcinas

Printed in Australia
DoctorZed Publishing rev. date: 21/01/2017